Also by Gary Paulsen

Picture books, illustrated by Ruth Wright Paulsen

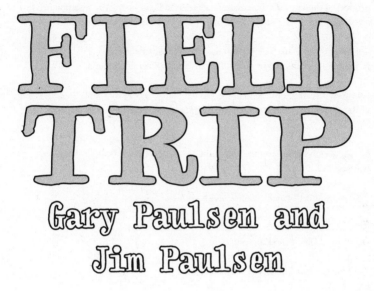

FIELD TRIP

Gary Paulsen and
Jim Paulsen

WENDY
LAMB
BOOKS

Text copyright © 2015 by James Paulsen and Gary Paulsen
Jacket photographs copyright © 2015 by Eric Isselee/Shutterstock

Visit us on the Web! randomhousekids.com

Educators and librarians, for a variety of teaching tools,
visit us at RHTeachersLibrarians.com

Library of Congress Cataloging-in-Publication Data
Paulsen, Gary.
    Field trip / Gary Paulsen and Jim Paulsen. – First edition.
        pages cm
    Sequel to: Road trip.
        ISBN 978-0-553-49674-1 (hardback) – ISBN 978-0-553-49675-8 (lib. bdg.) – ISBN 978-0-553-49676-5 (ebook)   [1. Fathers and sons–Fiction. 2. Automobile travel–fiction. 3. Border collie–Fiction. 4. Dogs–Fiction. 5. Brothers and sisters–Fiction. 6. Twins–Fiction. 7. Hockey–Fiction. 8. School field trips–Fiction.] I. Paulsen, Jim. II. Title.
    PZ7.P2843Fie 2015
    [Fic]–dc23

2014037288

The text of this book is set in 12-point Berthold Baskerville.
Interior design by Vikki Sheatsley

Printed in the United States of America
10 9 8 7 6 5 4 3 2 1
First Edition

Random House Children's Books supports the First Amendment and celebrates the right to read.

This book is dedicated to
Jonathan, Lori, Rebecca, and Jared
and to the good people at
Dog Patch,
A Place to Bark,
and Young at Heart,
who work tirelessly
to find good homes for
dogs in need.
Woof.

1

The Letters

I stagger in the back door after hockey, wrecked. Thursdays are brutal: strength and conditioning training for ninety minutes before school; then, after the last bell rings, back to the rink for a few hours on the ice. After twenty years of hard work (well, I'm fourteen, but ice time is way longer than real time), I finally made the best hockey team in town.

When I get home, all I want to do is eat and go to bed. A guy needs some peace and quiet. But peace and quiet are pretty rare at our house these days.

Last summer Dad suddenly quit his job as a corporate pencil pusher and started a business flipping houses. No, he's not a giant; flipping means he buys crummy places, fixes them up, and sells them. He's pretty good at what he does, I have to admit that; he's bought dumps that looked to me like nothing but rotting drywall and turned them into show houses.

But there's always the awful wait for the house to sell. And when Dad bugs out about things that are beyond his control, he rips apart something in *our* house.

For the past ten months, we've been living in a construction zone. When Dad's not at work, which is most of the time, he's home tearing down walls and pulling up floors.

Initially, I was really into Dad's company, Duffy and Son, and I worked for him last summer. But once I made the travel hockey team, I didn't have time for that. And I can't stand not having running water, and being able to see through the floor of my bedroom because Dad yanked up the boards. He and Mom love the constant remodeling—he thrives on the challenges, she enjoys the new stuff—but I hate it.

Today it's quiet when I get home. Just Atticus and Conor waiting for me. It's been this way for months—me and the guys. Sometimes I think they're the only ones who notice if I come home, and they're the main reasons I come home at all.

Atticus sneezes as I walk into the kitchen; the drywall dust bothers his nose. He's our fifteen-year-old border collie, and the construction makes him extra cranky.

Conor, the rescue puppy we adopted last summer,

caroms around the corner into the kitchen, sliding into the wall with a thump. His paws scrabble on the new hardwood floor—he hasn't gotten the hang of the slick wood yet—and he bats his stuffed lamb my way, to throw it for him to chase, but I kick it so the toy skids to him, pucklike. He pounces on it—goal denied! I have visions of putting together the world's first-ever canine hockey team. I am all hockey, all the time.

"Awesome defense, buddy." I try to get Conor to high-five me, but he tips over when he lifts a paw. He might be a little too clumsy for hockey. Atticus just watches the toy slide past him and then looks at me sadly. He'll catch Frisbees and balls, but hockey isn't his thing. Weird that we're related.

Atticus whines and stares at the slow cooker on the counter.

"Beef stroganoff today," I tell him. His ears prick up. I've been cooking for myself all year, and a slow cooker is a hungry guy's best friend. I had to start making my own meals after Mom took on the finances at Duffy and Son; she still works full-time at her old job, but now she takes care of our books in the evenings and on weekends. I looked up a bunch of easy recipes and started fending for myself. I don't know what Mom and Dad do about meals; I can't remember the last time we ate together.

I dump kibble in two bowls for the guys, then sit down with my plate of beefy noodles, and the three of us start inhaling supper. I look through the mail as I eat.

Two envelopes are addressed to *The Parents of Ben Duffy*. "My name is on them," I assure Atticus, who has stopped eating to watch me, his ears flattened in disapproval. "It's okay."

The first letter is from the assistant vice principal at my school. Atticus and Conor are nudging my thigh, so I read the letter to them. " 'Ben's attendance record is less than optimal.' That means I miss a lot of school because my hockey team has been red-hot this season and we've been invited to a bunch of tourneys and skills seminars," I explain. Atticus groans and lies down, and Conor scratches an itch behind his ear and falls over again. " 'Furthermore, he seems to be coasting in his classes, failing to live up to his full potential.' That's because I give everything I've got to the game. Duh."

Atticus sighs and rests his chin on my gear bag. He understands my priorities. Conor chews the bag's shoulder strap. He has yet to perfect supportive gestures the way Atticus has.

"Good thing I intercepted this note," I tell them. "It's the kind of thing that would worry Mom and Dad, and they have enough going on these days without school causing trouble. I know what I'm doing." Atticus tilts his head, doubtful. Conor snatches the letter from my hand. "That's what I think: out of sight, out of mind. Thanks, dude."

I open the second envelope. This letter is a lot more interesting, and I jump up and start pacing as I read because I'm so psyched. The guys follow me back and forth across the kitchen.

"Listen to this: 'Brookdale Hockey Academy is hosting invitational tryouts for the best and brightest hockey talent. Beginning this fall term, BHA will offer a live-in facility featuring a high-quality classroom education along with daily training for the country's highest-caliber student athletes. We are pleased to inform you that your son, Ben Duffy, has earned an invitation to apply for admission to our elite program.'"

My mind is racing. I've heard rumors about a place like this starting up a few hours away. I guess the academy is a go! And they want me! It's perfect—classes scheduled around practice, living and training with the best players, being coached by brilliant hockey minds. I'll finally be surrounded by people who get where my head is at and who will encourage my dream of playing pro someday. Not like Mom and Dad, who only nag me about leaving smelly gear in the kitchen and show up late to my games, when they can even make them.

Atticus paws at my leg, and Conor, who studies Atticus like he's going to be tested later, pounces on my shoe. I stop pacing and grin down at them.

"Best. News. Ever." Atticus makes a noise that sounds like *Noooooo,* but that can't be right: he's always got my back.

I turn my attention back to the letter. "Tryouts are this weekend! Acceptances are being announced next week. That's fast. Figures—hockey is the fastest game on earth. I have to call Coach, ask around to see if any of the other guys on the team are trying out, and arrange a ride."

"A ride where?" Dad comes in from the garage. He's carrying blueprints and paperwork; he must have bought a new house to flip. The Duffy family is on a winning streak today.

I'm so jazzed, I can't even find the words; I hand over the letter and wait for him to read the words that will change my life forever.

"Boarding school?" Dad frowns at the letter. "We never talked about you going away to school, much less a hockey academy." He makes air quotes when he says "academy," as if he doubts it's a real school. "Mom and I will have to talk this over, Ben. It's a big decision. Very expensive, too."

"It's not a decision, it's destiny. You know how hard I've been working and how I've . . . sacrificed." I wait and let that sink in; last summer Dad had to go back on his promise to let me go to hockey camp because of

6

the new business. It was a heartbreaker, but I joined a summer league in town and learned a lot, really upped my game. The disappointment about camp helped me develop new skills, and I've been working my butt off ever since. "Playing hockey is all I've dreamed of and worked for since I was five and got my first skates. Hockey's not just a game to me, Dad. It's what I love more than anything else in the world. And this is the opportunity of a lifetime."

"You said that about camp last summer. And the travel team last fall."

"Oh, uh, well, when you're a true-blue player like me, whose entire future revolves around hockey, you're bound to have more opportunities of a lifetime than average people." It's so hard to explain stuff like this to regular folks.

Before Dad can sit down and get caught up in the new house, I give it my best shot.

"I wish you knew what it feels like to be flying over the ice, working the puck, blowing past an opponent who looks like he's in slow motion, spotting the net, and then flipping your stick just right and sending the puck spinning past the goalie." I'm practically hyperventilating.

Dad's trying to listen, but he's sneaking glances at the blueprints on the table. This isn't the first time he's zoned out on me, thinking about boring stuff like money and bills, when I've been trying to tell him something important about the game. Mom does it, too.

I take a deep breath. Find the perfect words. "Hockey is the only thing I care about. It's all I think of. Hockey is my whole life—it's my future. I hope you keep that in mind when you talk to Mom."

I know enough to leave the room before I say something I'll regret. Like "Don't be a hypocrite, Dad—you're always talking about believing in yourself and how everything will work out if you just work hard enough." It may be the truth, but it'll torpedo my chances.

Besides, there's no way Mom and Dad won't let me go.

No. Way.

ATTICUS AND CONOR

Atticus: I don't want my boy to go away. He's too young, and I like my people bunched together so I can keep an eye on them. No one ever gets in trouble when I'm around, but when they go off in separate directions or try to keep secrets from me, things get weird. They don't seem to realize that; that's why I always try to keep my people close by.

As long as I can remember, it's been the boss and the real boss who smells like flowers and my boy and me. And now this falling-over puppy. My people need to spend more time together. Everyone is always coming and going and missing each other. My boy talks to me about everything, and he tries to explain things to the puppy, but he still needs to talk to the bosses. And they should listen better. Like I do.

They need to spend more time at home. I'm tired of taking care of this puppy. They wanted him, not me. The boss could stop messing the place up, too; it's always loud and dirty, and everything smells wrong.

Conor: I LOVE THE SHINY FLOOR! IT MAKES ME FLY!

The Decision

Dad drags me out of bed at five in the morning—his favorite time of the day to bring me up to speed on family disasters. He bounds down to the kitchen and as soon as I've staggered to the table, tells me that after careful consideration last night, he and Mom have decided not to let me try out for the new academy.

I brace myself against the counter and watch Dad pet Atticus, who glances at me and looks away quickly, horrified by the bomb Dad just dropped.

I struggle to control my quavering voice. "You can't do that to me."

"Sure I can; I'm your father and I have your best interests at heart."

"How long are you going to play that lame 'I'm the dad' card?"

"Can't see an end to it. Works like a charm."

"But you're wrong! You just don't get it. I'm four-teen, and these are crucial years for me. Every minute at the rink makes a difference. Don't you understand the importance of training with players and coaches who'll push me to be better every time I take the ice?"

I'm sweating and my hands are shaking, but Dad's sitting at the kitchen table calmly scratching the itch Atticus can't reach behind his right ear—arthritis in his hips has stiffened his back legs. Is Dad even listening to me or is he just waiting for me to stop talking? I press on.

"Any serious coach will tell you that turning down this kind of experience will trash the rest of my career and hold me back from any real momentum. Do you *want* to sentence me to a life of hockey mediocrity? Worst-case scenario? My game falls apart, my spirit is broken, and I walk away from the sport and . . . and . . . and I'm a bum living under an overpass!"

Dad tilts his head. "I think you're exaggerating."

"Barely."

"You've missed a ton of school this year for travel tournaments and clinics and camps and— Oh, hey, do you know anything about the letter Mom and I found under the kitchen table from the vice principal?"

I shrug. Dad raises an eyebrow. I should have known Conor wouldn't destroy the evidence. He's just a puppy, still learning; Atticus would have made sure there wasn't a scrap left.

"A good education," Dad is lecturing me now, "has to be your first priority, not shots on goal. Mom and I want you to explore opportunities, broaden your interests, attend a school with girls so you can go on dates, make friends who still have all their teeth.

"That's why I woke you up so early. Since you're going to be focusing less on skating from now on, you should go on your class field trip after all. It won't kill you to miss a few days of practice. Sure, the rest of the class left yesterday, but I'll drive you myself; we'll catch up to them in no time. We hit the road in a few minutes."

"What?" First he takes away my dream and then he makes me go on a nerdy field trip?

"It's going to be another amazing Dad and Ben On the Road Adventure."

I slump against the counter. What is it with Dad's new habit of springing catastrophic news at dawn and immediately dragging me on the road? He did it last summer when he ripped away hockey camp because he quit his job and started flipping houses. Then he whisked me away on a road trip. The good part was that we saved Conor, a rescue puppy in need of a home. And we met some great people. And had fun.

"ARFARFARFARFARF!" Conor chases his stuffed

lamb across the floor. He's the best thing to happen to this family in a long time, and I have to confess that our trip to get him didn't start out too well, either.

"Are we at least rescuing another puppy on the way?" I ask.

"You never know." Dad tries to sound mysterious, but I can tell he hadn't thought about a puppy until I mentioned it. He turns away and starts scrolling on his phone, searching for a puppy bribe.

Conor was promised to me last summer, but he took one look at Mom and fell in love. He's all hers. And Atticus has always belonged to Dad. Atticus and Conor like me just fine, but I get the feeling they think I'm a useful servant, not the reason they get up in the morning. I need a border collie of my own. I deserve one who loves me best.

A new puppy isn't going to make me forget about going to the academy, and I cringe at the idea of catching up with the field trip. But it'll take a while to reach the class snoozefest. Anything can happen between then and now.

The thought of a new puppy is enough to lift my crummy mood a little.

I catch Atticus's eye; he looks at Dad and then at Conor before turning back to me and wagging his tail to remind me what a great time we had on the last trip.

As usual, he has a point.

ATTICUS AND CONOR

Atticus: The boss has a good plan. Road trips are fun, and the boss and my boy will be together in the truck, talking, and then everything will work out in the end. Like it always does.

The boss also has a bad plan. Another puppy. I can barely stand this one—he's not coming around like I thought he would.

My boy and the boss and the real boss, the one who smells like flowers, like this puppy. At first I thought he had potential. But he's making us look bad, with all his barking and rolling around. It's loud. Undignified. He trips over his own paws. I pretend I don't notice and look away.

I might be too old to raise two puppies. Puppies are a lot of work.

But anything can happen once the boss gets on the road; he could forget about the puppy. He does forget things.

Conor: A PUPPY! I've always wanted a puppy! Puppies are easy, not like Atticus, who is crabby and just likes to sleep in the sun. I'M GOING TO GET A PUPPY!

3

The Ultimate Flip
and the Stowaway

As I'm grabbing some clothes for the trip, I do some deep breathing exercises I use when game pressure is on. I regroup: how to swing things back in my favor? It's third period, Duffy; the score's tied one-all. You've got one last chance to take control of the game.

Less hockey? We'll see about that. I'll figure out how to show Dad how badly I want this and convince him what a great deal the academy is.

Wait! *That's* what this is all about. Dad's just testing me—he's making me *earn* the academy. He wants to make sure I've thought this through. If I prove myself on the road and I don't moan and I'm a team player about the field trip, he'll be so impressed he'll let me try out. Yeah! Dad's not the only one who thinks everything will work out in the end.

My brain is starting to whir. Always have a Plan B—Dad taught me that. I'm feeling better already. Gordie Howe would never let a setback like this get the best of him; neither will I.

I shove my dog-eared Wayne Gretzky autobiography and my team playbook into my bag. Out of habit, I grab my hockey bag, too. Feels weird to go anywhere without it.

I head back to the kitchen with a bounce in my step. I'll get some studying done in the truck, a visual aid to impress Dad.

"Oh, uh, Ben," Dad says in a voice I've only heard once before: when he told me he'd bought us a crack house in a really dicey area to fix up. I try to catch his eye. He's not looking at me. "I have some, uh, news."

"More?" I brace myself for the second time this morning.

"It's good—don't look so worried. It's great, actually. It may well be the best thing that ever happened to this family!"

Wow. This is bad. Really bad.

"I sold another house. One I wasn't even trying to sell: I'm *that* good! Ha ha ha."

At Dad's fake laugh, I close my eyes. This will be genuinely hideous.

"I sold *our* house!"

"You *what*?" If I weren't gripping the countertop, I'd keel over.

"I was as surprised as you are."

"Oh. You accidentally sold our house. Sure, happens all the time. You read about it in the newspaper, see stories on the news." I roll my eyes.

Atticus and Conor slink to the kitchen door and stand with their backs to us, probably hoping one or the other will suddenly sprout hands so they can work the doorknob and escape.

"I know. Crazy, right?" Dad's sticking with cheerful. "I sank a ton of money into that old place on Calhoun and Harriet. More than I expected. I needed money fast to keep the project on track."

"So you sold our family home. Right out from underneath us. Without consulting us." I just want to be clear.

"Yeah!" Dad nods, glad that I get it. "The good news is that I turned such a profit it would have been criminal to let the offer go. The buyer came to me, like the universe was helping me take the business to the next level. Plus, now I can get the Calhoun place up to code and make it a masterpiece. The profit we're going to see on that place, Ben . . ."

"What about us? Where are we going to live? When do we move? What did Mom say? Does she even know?"

"Of course she knows."

"And . . . ?"

"She's going to hammer out some details while we're gone." Dad nods happily.

"Details. You mean like packing everything we own and, oh, finding us a new place to live?"

"Yup! I'm not good with the particulars. I'm a big-picture guy." Dad's foot is tapping under his chair and he's drumming his fingers on the tabletop, antsy to get going now that he's dumped the news. "She was up half the night looking for the new Casa Duffy online."

Traitor. I glare at the ceiling and Mom still asleep upstairs. "She used to worry about the way you run the business," I remind him.

"That was before she started doing the bookkeeping. Now she's behind me a hundred percent!"

Atticus barks at me. Sounds like "Go." Conor's still staring at the back door, willing it to open.

At least some of us are excited to hit the road.

I shuffle out to the pickup, two border collies hot on my heels. Atticus and Conor go everywhere with us—if we try to escape, they aren't above tripping us to remind us to bring them along. I feel bad for sheep when I see how ruthlessly border collies herd their people.

"Not the pickup, Ben," Dad calls as he locks the back door. "We're taking the company car."

No. Freaking. Way.

The company car . . . Dad told us he was going to buy a van for next to nothing at a sheriff's auction. Mom and I thought that made sense. But then he brought home an old ice cream van with a ginormous chipped fiberglass swirl cone cemented to the roof. It used to be pink-and-white stripes but has turned a deadly gray. Dad's crazy about the cone and all the space on the inside. He said no one else saw the fun of driving around underneath an oversized plastic ice cream cone. I am one of those people.

So I throw my duffel in the back of the van as hard as I can because not only do I have to prove myself and make him let me go to hockey school, but now I have to do it underneath the Death Cone.

"Umph." A pile of tarps on one of the seats groans and moves as my gear lands. I jump back. Atticus growls and slides between the van and me; Conor yelps and runs in circles around me—he hasn't figured out the appropriate response to possible danger.

"Oh, hey, Brig," Dad says, glancing past me at the sleepy-faced guy crawling out of the van. He could be anywhere from seventeen to, um, twenty-four? "Did we wake you?"

Atticus and Conor bark and jump on the guy, greeting him like an old friend. He's got shaggy hair and is wearing baggy work pants and hiking boots and a ratty tee that reads DUFFY AND SON. We have company shirts now? He's super skinny but strong; even both guys throwing themselves at him doesn't take him off his feet.

"Yeah, thanks. Not a bad wake-up call. My alarm clock is too loud and always makes the cone on the roof vibrate." Brig rubs his eyes, stretches, and yawns. "Hey, buddy," he says to Atticus and Conor as they scramble to get him to pet them. Even Atticus is all over him. Shockingly out of character.

"Some info would be nice," I say to Dad. Are we going to be fighting for sleeping space in our vehicles now that we have no home?

"This is Brig."

"Uh-huh . . . ?"

"My apprentice."

"Really." I hope sarcasm is a sustainable natural resource, because I'd hate to run out. I can see that bitter derision is going to be my default response to everything Dad shares from now on.

"Apprentice, assistant, paid intern, associate, craftsman, what have you. Duffy and Son is an up-and-coming business with multiple employees." Dad beams.

"Hey, nice to meet you." Brig stops petting my border collies long enough to shake my hand. "Mr. Duffy told me all about you. I'm Brigham Hancock."

"Good to meet you, Brig. Do you always sleep in Dad's van?"

"Ever since I started working for him."

"Why?"

"So that I'm never late for work. I love my job, and I'd hate to disappoint Mr. Duffy. I'm on call for him twenty-four/seven."

"Did you know this, Dad?" He's looking at a map. Why, I have no idea; it's not like he uses them. I don't even know why he owns any. It's like a killer whale buying ballet slippers—they're just never going to come in handy.

"I know Brig loves working for me. I didn't know he was sleeping in the van."

Geez. This day is so weird.

"You don't usually need the van so early," Brig says.

"Getting my boy to his class field trip, taking his mind off a bad idea, maybe getting a puppy. Who knows? The day is young."

"Your dad is teaching me the business. And how to multitask." Brig gazes at Dad with admiration.

"Yeah, Dad's super good at doing more than one thing at a time." Look at how he left me homeless and destroyed my career. Is it really less than an hour since I was asleep, with a fixed address and a great future ahead of me?

Atticus growls at Conor, and Conor falls off the seat in the van.

"Well, let's go," Brig says. "The guys are restless." He climbs back into the van and shoves the pile of junk he was sleeping on off the seat, urging Conor away from Atticus and showing Atticus that his space is his again. Atticus is territorial and likes to sit next to the sliding window where kids used to buy Bomb Pops and Fudgsicles and Dream Bars. Dad added removable seats and a couple of shelves and ceiling hooks for his tools and gear, but he left the order window and the freezer and all the other equipment in place. I wouldn't be surprised if he starts selling frozen treats just because he can. He'd think it was awesome.

Brig and the border collies look expectantly at Dad and me: *Go!*

"Brig's coming, too?" I ask Dad as we climb into the front seats.

Dad turns the key in the ignition. "We're kind of taking his bedroom with us, and if I'm not around, there's no work, so why not? Look how much fun we had last year when we took on passengers. It's a good thing we ignore that rule about not picking up strangers." He nods, proud of our family's eagerness to flout the basic standards of safety.

"Mr. Duffy picked me up when I was hitchhiking," Brig tells me. "Convinced me not to run away, said I should stick around, work for him, make something of my life. But I'm sure you know the whole story."

I didn't know you existed until ten minutes ago, I think, but I nod.

"He's like the dad I never had." Brig smiles.

Hunh. Well, I'm sure you're like the son he never had, too, if you love working for him so much you sleep in the van. "That's . . . nice," I finally say.

The Duffys belong to a national rescue group that fosters border collies; did Dad join one for runaway teens, too? He has a thing for strays.

"Brig coming along is a good omen, Ben. Can't you feel it?" Dad asks.

I feel resentment, anxiety, and the hot, slobbery breath of Conor on the back of my neck.

When Dad, Atticus, and I set out to rescue Conor last summer, it was just the three of us, and I was super ticked-off at him. But on the way to the shelter we picked up a teen hoodlum, a cranky mechanic, and a runaway waitress. By the time we got home, we'd become a weird little road family, and Dad and I were getting along great. I can tell by the way Dad's smiling at Brig and the dogs in the rearview mirror that he thinks the same thing is going to happen this time. I guess he's never heard that lightning doesn't strike twice in the same place. I almost feel a little bad for him.

"Well, it's not like we don't have room for more people." I sigh.

Dad slaps his thigh. "I almost forgot! We have to make a quick stop and pick up the twins."

Of course we do. We need a set of twins.

All righty then.

ATTICUS AND CONOR

Atticus: I'm always on the boss's side. Even though he changes his mind too fast and too many times, he's usually right.

But he may have gone too far this time. Our new home might have a lot of stairs that will hurt my hips when I climb them, and small windows so there aren't nice patches of sun on the floor where I can sleep.

We should stay where we are. We could send this puppy to a new place and keep the boy who works for the boss. He's coming along nicely, settling in with the family. My boy didn't notice him until today, so he'll need some time to adjust.

And we're getting more new people now. That's good. The boss and the boy never fight in front of people. They try harder to get along when they're not alone. We should have had company last night when the boss and the real boss were talking. Well, he talked and she sat there quiet and then went for a walk. Not the good kind, where she takes us. The stompy kind without us.

Conor: I'M GOING BUH-BYE IN THE VAN!!!!

The Twins

"So, Dad, care to share deets on the twin thing?" I hope he's noticing how awesome I'm being: calm, easygoing, curious, open to new people and experiences. The perfect son to send to Brookdale Hockey Academy.

"Jacob and Charlotte Norton. Great kids. But you know that. They're in your class."

They are? Maybe Dad is right about hockey taking over my brain, because I can't connect these names with faces. In my defense, at school I focus on getting my homework done ahead of time so I don't have it hanging over my head when I hit the ice. Distraction is not good for elite players. Neither is fatigue, so I can't stay up late hanging out with friends or doing homework. I can name every player on every Stanley Cup–winning team for the past forty years, and I know every hockey player my age and at my level in the country who might be competition or a teammate when I turn pro, but I'm not too sure who most of the kids at school are.

"Oh, sure, Jacob and Charlotte Norton," I bluff. "So why are we picking them up?"

"They had to go to a funeral yesterday and couldn't leave with your class. I called their dad last night about a job and he was bummed that they had to miss the class trip, seeing as how Charlotte is the student council president and Jacob is the class representative to the parent-teacher association and they did most of the work to make the trip happen—the museum passes, chaperones, lesson plans connected to the museum exhibits . . . you know, stuff like that."

Oh, right. Jacob and Charlotte. The kind of Super-Involved Students teachers and administrators wish they could clone. A vague picture comes to mind of people who play in the band; sing in the choir; act in the plays; join numerous teams; win state contests in essay writing, science experiments, and social studies projects; host foreign exchange students; spearhead fundraisers for food pantries; wash cars to raise awareness of air pollution or endangered species or something; and volunteer at nursing homes, reading to old folks. Them. Snore.

Dad is still talking. ". . . so that's when I knew: Ben can't pass up this awesome experience because (a) it's a once-in-a-lifetime chance, and (b) the payments are non-refundable. And Jacob and Charlotte shouldn't miss it. Ben, it was like a call from the universe—another one, like selling the house."

This day just keeps getting better: He's hearing cosmic orders. I open the glove box and root around for licorice or jelly beans. A sugar buzz will help me cope.

"Hey, Ben." Brig taps my shoulder. "Can you hand me the box of Red Hots your dad keeps on the dash? My breath is freaking Conor out because I just ate sardines and leftover garlic stir-fry for breakfast. I tried to share, but he didn't want any."

"Can't have a freaked-out border collie." I hand back the candy and gag at the stench. I try not to compare Brig's consideration of Conor's comfort level with Dad's lack of concern about the security and future of his only son. I crack the window for some fresh air, tip my head back, and close my eyes. I should learn to meditate.

A few minutes later we pull over and I see two kids standing in a driveway. They have matching backpacks and duffel bags and are wearing pressed cargo pants, brand-new hiking boots, and matching T-shirts with the name of our school on the front. They're waving and grinning, oozing enthusiasm and pep. I sigh. Here come the twintastics.

"Hi, Mr. Duffy." The girl climbs in the back next to Brig and the border collies. She's wearing glasses and has her hair in a ponytail. "I got up early and made sugar- and fat-free power muffins for us. Bran buds, organic cranberries, protein powder, free-range eggs from the chickens I raise. For moistness, I made applesauce from the tree in our backyard instead of using shortening, which, according to current research, is lethal."

She hands a muffin to Brig, who pulls a can out of his bag, dips two fingers in, and smears confetti frosting on the muffin. Charlotte flinches.

"Hi, Charlotte," I jump in. "Thanks for the muffins, very . . . thoughtful of you." I'd kill for something deep-fried or oozing with melted cheese, but she looks so disappointed with Brigham that I want to make her feel better. "That's Brig. He works with my dad. He's got, um, low blood sugar and will pass out if he doesn't eat frosting." She seems skeptical, but she smiles at me. Whoa. Great smile. Didn't expect a girl like her to be so cute.

"I'm Ben—"

Brig pulls a can out of his bag and tips it in his mouth for a whipped-cream chaser.

I shudder and continue. "—and the younger border collie is Conor and the other one is Atticus." Both of the guys are staring at her muffin and drooling. She breaks it in two pieces, giving half to each. Atticus gulps his down whole, but Conor chews, gacks, and spews chewed-up muffin on Charlotte's shirt. Before

I can apologize, she whips a box of wet wipes and a stain stick out of her backpack and starts de-crumbing and un-goobering her shirt. She's not mad, though; she laughs and pets Conor, who tries to help her by licking the goo off. She's pretty mellow about dog spit. "I like your truck," she tells me. The Death Cone becomes a little cooler in my eyes if she approves.

Jacob settles into the far backseat. Before I can say anything to him, Dad says, "Let's get started," and throws the van in reverse. He zooms out of the drive-way and, once in the street, makes a sickening lurch into forward gear. Conor, who hasn't gotten the hang of driving with Dad, crashes into the back of my seat, wag-ging his tail like this is a fun new game. Atticus looks as dignified as a statue, immune to petty forces like mo-mentum and gravity. Atticus glances at Conor to make sure he's okay before, I swear, rolling his eyes and then looking out the window. Atticus spends a lot of his time pretending the rest of us aren't embarrassing him.

Conor crawls between the two front seats, poking his black-and-white snout between Dad and me, and howls in excitement. Dad gives a howl of his own, Brig barks a few times, and Jacob and Charlotte give a few shy yips, trying to fit in. Atticus sneezes in disgust. Oh, what the heck: I punch the button to make the ice cream truck song play out of the speakers.

We're officially under way.

ATTICUS AND CONOR

Atticus: The dry food blob the girl shared was horrible. But the puppy should have swallowed it. If you spew food back at people, they don't give you more. Sometimes they take you to the vet. And they don't share the next time they eat. We always get hamburgers on the road, but the puppy might not get one now. That's okay; I'll eat it.

I like bringing more people with us. The muffin girl and her boy sit behind me, and the boy who works with the boss lets me sit in my spot.

My boy can't stop looking at the girl.

Conor: WE HAVE NEW FRIENDS!!!!! WITH TERRIBLE TREATS!!!!

The Two Points of View

"You must be Jacob," I call to the boy in the back. "Sorry about the puppy puke."

"No problem." He beams. "This is the greatest day of my life. Everything that happens is perfect and exactly the way it's meant to be."

Atticus and I look at each other. Right. In a past life, Jacob was probably super stoked about that snazzy new ship the *Titanic*.

"Today is the greatest day of his life since yesterday," Charlotte clarifies, and smiles at Jacob. I like her more all the time.

"Yesterday was pretty awesome," Jacob agrees. "A personal best for learning new stuff. I went to Great-Aunt Pansy's funeral. Did you know that morticians insert a tube into the abdomen of a deceased body? After which a pump is attached so that the contents of the stomach and intestines can be pumped out? This also removes all of the gases from the body and prevents bloating."

"Wow," I say. He's not boring and dweeby at all.

"Jacob thinks every day is the best day of his life." Charlotte looks at me and Brig. "And that no information is too gross."

"Uh-huh," I say. We'll see about that after he's spent some time with Brig and his bag of horrible food.

"Can I tell you something?" Jacob asks. I nod. "This is the greatest day of your life, too!"

I'm pretty sure he's wrong, but there's something about his goofy grin that makes me fake an encouraging expression. "Keep talking."

"You're traveling with an international star in the making and a future household name in politics. Journalists will contact you in years to come to confirm that you knew us back in the day."

I must look confused. "Charlotte's going to run the world someday, and I'm going to entertain it. We're . . ."

He can't think of the word, so I supply: "Twincredible!"

"Exactly! We've heard our callings at a young age; we discovered our gifts and we know how we want to spend the rest of our lives. Charlotte and I have worked like crazy to prepare for our futures." I know about that. I punch Dad to make sure he's listening.

"I couldn't agree with you more. Sounds, oh, I don't know, Really Super Familiar, don't you think, Dad? A serious lifetime goal at fourteen?" I'm happy to see Dad shift uncomfortably in his seat.

"Tell me, Jacob," Dad suddenly says in that fake-cheerful voice he uses when he's trying to get something he wants but also seem like a nice guy doing it, "what kind of extracurriculars are you and your sister involved in, and aren't you in all the high-level classes?"

I zone out and glare at the passing road signs as Jacob talks. Our school has that many teams and clubs? Dial it back, buddy.

"Impressive," I lie when Jacob is finished with his list, "but don't you worry that you're the jack-of-all-trades, master of none?" I heard someone say that to Dad at a job site once and, from the way he screwed up his mouth, I could tell it wasn't a good thing.

"Oh, no. See, at our age, it's all about exposure to a variety of options and taking advantage of as many opportunities as we can," Charlotte says.

"Now, doesn't that sound Really Super Familiar, Ben?" Dad smirks.

I glance back in the mirror on my visor; Charlotte and Jacob are leaning forward in their seats, eyes glowing. Brig is asleep, I think; it's me against . . . everybody.

"Ben wants to transfer to a new school, if you can even call it a school," Dad says sadly, as if I told him I'm going to join an expedition to pillage the Amazon rain forest. "It's a new hockey academy. He'll concentrate on power plays and become well educated in blade sharpening and stick handling. He'll never go to a school dance, his only friends will be puck jockeys, he won't learn calculus or read Shakespeare, and he'll have a frequent-flyer card at the emergency room, probably learn to give himself stitches with black thread and a sewing needle."

"But, Dad! You haven't been listening to everything I've been saying! You're missing the big picture I have in mind. The hockey academy is only the first step. Plus, they teach how to avoid injuries. If I do well there the next four years—and it *is* a real school with normal high school subjects—I'm bound to be recruited by some awesome college. I won't go professional until after I have a diploma. I have it all worked out."

The man who quit his job and cashed in his retirement fund to buy a crack house to renovate, and who just unloaded our house, looks at me and shakes his head. Like crazy self-determination doesn't run in the family.

"You make some good points," Charlotte says.

"Who?" Dad and I ask at the same time.

"Both of you."

"But I have the more compelling argument," Dad sits up. "I'm the dad, and what I say goes."

"Unquestioned patriarchal authority is one of the least effective, not to mention most unpopular, forms of leadership." Charlotte is brisk. "It's not a valid way to participate in a healthy family. The keystone of democracy is everyone's right to freely express their opinions, avoiding an abuse of power by autocratic rulers."

Charlotte winks at me. I turn to Dad. "Sounds to me like 'because I say so' is an assault on basic human rights." He sighs.

"Plus, it's no way to have the best day ever," Jacob adds. "I've always found that people who insist on getting their way despite the good ideas of others don't last long in sports. Or on the stage. Or in committee work. It's better to compromise."

"You compromise at work, Mr. Duffy." Guess Brig wasn't sleeping. "You're always respectful about asking my opinion on the job."

Charlotte and I lean way out across Brig and Atticus and bump fists. This trip has taken a big step in the right direction.

I stretch, sit back, and watch the scenery whiz by.

"But," Charlotte says, "there is something to be said for the judgment and experience of an elder, whose duty is to place his or her wisdom and knowledge at the service of the greater good."

Say what? My head snaps around.

Dad sits up a little straighter in the driver's seat.

"And every team I've ever been on only has one coach," Jacob says.

Dad grins.

"And I've never known Mr. Duffy to screw up," Brig offers. "Well, I mean, we screw up all the time, but he always figures out how to fix it."

I sigh and look out the window.

Brig dips a beef jerky stick in the can of frosting to scrape out the last bit, singing along to the song on the radio. Charlotte starts reading a book as she scratches a blissed-out Conor's tummy. Atticus is peering out the window, ready to lead us back home when Dad gets us lost. Jacob fiddles with the busted soft-serve machine on the van wall.

Charlotte looks up from her book and smiles at me. My stomach flips and I smile back.

I'm not going to say this out loud, because it's the kind of thing Dad would never let me forget, but I suspect he might have some kind of magnetism that attracts interesting people.

It's kinda cool.

And at least I'm in good company while I try to figure out how to salvage my life.

ATTICUS AND CONOR

Atticus: I'm the only one who seems to know that the boss is never going to catch up to the field trip like he says. He's already turned around three times. I don't think anyone has noticed. They're too busy talking to pay attention.

Conor: Snore.

The Plot and
the First Diversion

Everyone's fallen asleep in the back. Hockey players are practically bionic, so I'm wide-awake. But bored. Dad might not read maps, but I do. I'm tracing the route we seem to be on when a town catches my attention.

I can't immediately tell why the name rings a bell. I'm absentmindedly shuffling an old puck in my hand when it hits me: the name on the letter from the academy. Tryouts are at that town's rink. I reach for my phone and look it up. Yup. Tryouts. Tomorrow.

I wonder . . .

We're going to pass right through the town where the recruiters will be looking for my kind of talent. Dad's not the only one who gets signs from the universe. Whatever has been whispering to Dad has a message for me, too. *Ben, try out.*

If I can show Dad how impressed the admissions people are by my skills, he can't say no. He hasn't seen me play in a while, so he's not up to speed on how awesome I am. And words won't work—our last conversation proved that. I have to show him.

I just have to figure out how get us to the rink tomorrow on the sly, because if I ask him to take me, he'll shut me down.

I need a distraction that'll keep us busy for the rest of the day so we can show up at the right time tomorrow.

Something will come up; it always does. All I have to do is keep my eyes open and think positive thoughts.

Dad hits the brakes with a sickening jolt.

"What was that for?" I'm not proud of the way my voice cracks, but no one seems to notice. And Charlotte was switching seats with Brig when she was thrown forward. She reaches out to grab my shoulder to steady herself. My skin tingles under her hand.

"Look over there." Dad's tone is reverent, hushed. We all look where he's pointing.

"What are we looking at?" Jacob asks.

"I don't see anything." Charlotte tries to nudge Atticus aside so she can get a better view.

"I'll get the petty cash box," Brig breathes, as thrilled as Dad.

"What's happening?" Jacob asks.

"Dad spotted an estate sale." Just the time-suck I was hoping for. Score!

"What's that?"

"It's what fancy people call a garage sale for suckers like Dad. Some people can't resist buying bargain crap from other people's houses."

Dad unbuckles his seat belt and opens the van door, in a trance, heading toward the yard full of junk with a glassy-eyed stare. I climb out, crossing my fingers that he'll spend hours looking around.

Brig jogs ahead, a cigar box of money under his arm. Charlotte and Jacob follow me and the guys. I glance down—Atticus is depressed because he hates shopping, but Conor prances. He lacks the boredom gene. Everything is fun for him. And maybe he agrees with Dad that some million-dollar treasure can be snapped up for seventy-five cents.

I see Jacob's and Charlotte's perplexed expressions. "Dad's always looking for stuff for his flip houses. Just watch—he's going to get all jazzed about buying a mason jar full of nuts and bolts for a quarter, or he's going to find a like-new toilet." We all cringe at the thought of sharing the back of the van with that.

We stand on the curb with the guys, watching Dad and Brig cruise the card tables.

"I don't get it," Charlotte finally says.

"Lucky you. I don't tell many people this, but Dad also Dumpster dives. He knows the schedule for all the neighborhood's garbage and recycling pickup days, and he drives up and down streets looking for odds and ends he can fix up or use. 'One man's trash is another man's treasure,' Dad always says."

"We're never going to catch up with the field trip, are we?" Charlotte sounds more curious than disappointed.

"Well . . . follow-through isn't Dad's strong suit." Dad won't forget about the puppy though, right? Nah, puppies and field trips are two completely different things. One you can live without just fine, but not even Dad can space out about a puppy.

"Okay by me," Jacob says. "I'm kind of bored with the field trip from all the planning. We'll make our own educational experience, an independent study. I'll get back to you with a plan."

"No, you won't." Charlotte shakes her head. "I'm more organized. I'll figure out an alternative."

"You're organized, but I'm creative."

I jump in. "Why don't you both think about it and we'll talk about it later." Or never.

Conor chases a squirrel into the yard next door.

I whistle to call him back to my side. "That place is condemned." I point to the bright orange notification on the front door. "They're probably going to knock it down."

"What do you mean 'knock it down'?" Brig is standing nearby sorting scrap wood. "You mean that a space that's sheltered families, witnessed generations of laughter and tears, births and deaths, is going to be destroyed?" He sinks to the curb, like the news is too much to take.

Brig is panting and wild-eyed and raking his fingers through his hair. It's kind of scary. Our goalie, Dooter, looked like that during last year's regionals. Of course, his tibia was poking through his shin.

Jacob pats Brig's shoulder and Charlotte speaks to him softly. I dig in his backpack and come up with a can of squirtable cheese and some oatmeal raisin cookies. After a couple of cookie sandwiches, Brig calms down.

"I just feel so awful for the house," he mumbles through a mouthful.

"Well, sure . . ." I'm not sure how to comfort someone who gets so upset about drywall and shingles.

Dad, who didn't seem to notice when he ripped my soul to pieces earlier, spots Brig's distress. To be fair, Atticus alerted him.

"What's going on?" Dad looks at me suspiciously.

I throw my hands out in the "I'm innocent" gesture.

Conor crawls onto Brig's lap. Atticus solemnly puts a paw on Brig's knee, the silent message being *Pull yourself together, man. We're in public.*

Brig sniffs, wiping his nose on Conor's fur. "That

beautiful house, relegated to the scrap heap because it got a little old, a little run-down. It's tragic how we're becoming a disposable society."

"I couldn't agree with you more," Dad says. In the game of crazy poker, Dad will always see your hysteria and raise you an exaggeration.

Atticus and I catch each other's eyes and sigh. We've heard Dad's speech. Atticus lies down and pretends to take a nap. I look at Charlotte and Jacob and shake my head, silently warning them. Brig looks at Dad like he's waiting for the Rapture.

"I save old houses because I believe it's vital to protect the past. I restore venerable beauties who've seen better days to their former glories, protecting and defending the memories that live within those walls." This is the point in his speech where Dad pauses, as if choked up, and takes a deep breath. If you haven't heard it a million times, it's effective. Brig bites his lip and blinks hard. Charlotte and Jacob listen politely as Dad winds up. "I know this: it's not just a house, it's a home."

Brig stands and throws his arms around Dad. "It's a beautiful thing, what we do. Rock on." He turns to fist-bump me. "We have the best dad!"

" 'We'?" And you lack boundaries, I think, but force a smile.

"Brig thinks he's family," Jacob whispers to me. "Let

me know if you need any pointers on sibling rivalry. Charlotte and I have been competing since we were born."

"Before we were born," she says. "I'm seven minutes older, and I've been ahead of you since you were a two-celled organism developing in my shadow."

She pulls her tablet out of her bag, starting to swipe and type furiously.

"Let's get a better look at that house." Dad studies the front door.

"Why not?" I ask. "Luckily, my tetanus booster is up to date." If I weren't trying to run the clock out today, there's no way I'd encourage Dad to break into a padlocked house full of rusty nails and feral, rabid animals just to check out the crown molding and doorframes he'd like to pry out and reuse.

"It's got a very welcoming air about it, don't you think?" Dad and Brig run off and the rest of us drift after.

"Yeah," I say. "The windows boarded up with plywood sheets spray-painted with large black Xs just scream 'Come on in and set a spell.'"

Jacob and Charlotte crack up, but Dad can't hear me. He grabs the padlock on the front door and gives it a shake. "Nope." Then he heads toward the backyard, pointing to Brig to check the boards nailed across the windows.

"I'm in!" Jacob calls from the depths of the house. He's shimmied through a hole in the back door. He twists the lock from the inside and jumps out of the way when the door falls off the frame.

"Nicely done, Jacob." Dad and Brig high-five him. Charlotte and I tiptoe inside, stepping on a layer of trash. I can tell Charlotte shares my fear of sharp objects and wild animals. Dad is snapping pictures of the kitchen cabinets with his phone.

"This house obviously wasn't condemned because of structural faults." Dad looks around. "Every issue, as far as I can see, is mostly cosmetic. The foundation looks solid. Another example of someone letting a house go rather than putting in the elbow grease to make it shine."

"This house has got a really good spirit," Brig says to me. "Your dad taught me how to read a space, and this one has a happy soul. Can't you feel it?"

"I'm, uh, not sure." He looks so disappointed that I say, "Right, the energy. Yeah, it's good."

Charlotte hops onto a counter and studies her tablet. Before I can say anything about putting down the electronics and being present in the moment, which I hear a lot at home, Dad calls.

"Do you see what I see?" Jacob, Brig, Atticus, Conor, and I crowd the doorway.

"A built-in buffet," Brig breathes. "In mint condition."

Dad snaps more pictures and Brig runs his hands over the wood.

I read their minds. "It won't fit in the van. Not with four people and the two guys. There's no room."

Dad looks at me, his face aglow. "If we take out the benches and stack them along one side of the van, the buffet will fit perfectly."

"Remove the seats? With four people and two border collies?"

"Three people. You've been sitting in the front with me. Atticus and Conor don't mind lying on the floor. We'll bunch up a few tarps for the twins and Brig. They'll think they're sitting in beanbag chairs. It'll all work out."

"I'll go get the toolbox." Brig heads to the truck.

"And you two"—Dad points to Jacob and me—"see if you can jimmy the front door open and then grab some skids from the back of the van to make a ramp down the front steps. We'll just ease this baby out of the wall and slide it down the stairs, and it'll float into the van."

Uh-huh. I think gravity has different ideas. But since (a) I'm the Perfect Son Dad Will Want to Send to Hockey School and (b) this is a project that'll keep us here for hours, I start yanking plywood off the front door.

A curse-filled, unproductive, painful hour passes. Charlotte's still working on her tablet in the kitchen.

I have a vision of Charlotte, Jacob, Brig, Conor, Atticus, and me lashed to the side of the Death Cone on the roof for the rest of the trip if we ever do get this monstrosity into the van.

"Well." Charlotte dances up to us gleefully, "I did it!"

"Did what?" I rub the sweat off my face.

"Bought the house."

"Uh, what?"

"I didn't get why Mr. Duffy and Brig were so interested in this house, but when you said that he could tell how special it was, I finally understood."

"You did?" She's looking at me with a great smile, and there's nothing I would say to make her stop looking at me that way, so I keep my mouth shut.

"I found out this house was foreclosed on and went up for auction, but no one bid. I was able to buy it for a buck!"

"You bought a whole house for a dollar? How did a kid buy a house?" And why isn't Dad snatching up bargains like this?

"Charlotte can do anything online." Jacob beams. "She could be a great criminal or computer hacker if she wanted to. But she only uses her powers for good. Borrrrring."

"I didn't buy the house for myself. I just found out it was for sale and located the perfect buyer and did the legwork for them to make the offer." Even Dad looks astonished, so she explains, "I volunteer for a foundation that helps financially challenged homeowners buy cheap houses and fix them up. They said I should make an offer right away after I told them about the place and how sound you said it was. They'll be here tomorrow to show the place to prospective homeowners."

"And to think how close we were to ripping its heart out." Brig shakes his head, a little free with the word "we," if you ask me. "Good thing the buffet is still in place."

"Yeah, good thing." I stick a fresh Band-Aid on the gash on my arm. Hockey players know how to play through pain. Gonna have to ice my smashed toes tonight so I can shove my foot in my skate tomorrow.

Tomorrow.

I forgot about my plan for a while. We haven't chewed up nearly enough time to keep us on my secret schedule. I look around frantically.

"This place is filthy and disgusting," I announce. "Dad always says that first impressions are crucial." Dad pats my shoulder. "We should make a few simple repairs before the foundation people show up. Even for a dollar, this place looks overpriced."

Brig lights up. "Dibs on repairing those doors, Dad. I mean, Mr. Duffy."

Dad? How'd Brig and Dad get so tight? I shoot a quick look out the front door to make sure the truck still reads DUFFY & SON and not DUFFY & SONS or maybe even DUFFY & BRIG.

"Grab some trash bags and work gloves, Ben," Dad tells me. "You and Charlotte start picking up all the garbage. Jacob and I will take the plywood off the windows."

"The former owners ate a ton of fast food." Charlotte looks around. I take a second to ask the universe not to find bugs or rats. I'm only brave in the face of physical danger; gross things freak me out. Screaming because a cockroach skitters across my feet won't make Charlotte think I'm awesome.

"I move like greased lightning," I warn her. "The blur you'll see—that'll be me." We grab gloves and face masks from Dad's supplies and get to work.

I didn't expect that picking up rotten pizza boxes and moldy fried chicken buckets would be such a great way to get to know a girl. I wish she played hockey because we work together so well. Jacob wasn't kidding when he said Charlotte was competitive; she could go one on one with the toughest guy in my league. We race each other to sweep the house clean of garbage. We don't even have to talk; we just hustle. She is the coolest girl ever.

Dad and Brig crawl into the attic. Charlotte and I wash windows. Jacob sweeps. We tighten door hinges, nail down loose floorboards, dump bleach in the toilets. I'm sweating like a pig and covered in a thick layer of crud. Charlotte just gets prettier and prettier; her hair comes out of her ponytail and her cheeks get pink.

"Aha!" Jacob comes out of the kitchen, waving Charlotte's tablet. "My sister isn't the only one who can do an online search. I called the local television station and they're going to do a feel-good piece about how the house was saved and will be a fresh start for a family in need!"

Charlotte pretends to be annoyed with him for trying to one-up her, but I can see the smile she tries to hide. "Jacob thinks good deeds are nothing without publicity."

"All this work should be a secret?" he asks. "Look around—we did an amazing job."

The way Charlotte throws her arm around my shoulders as we study our efforts almost makes up for the little stab of jealousy I feel when I hear Dad tell Brig "Good job." He doesn't say a word to me.

Brig seems to be replacing me. On the bright side, Brig will keep Dad company when I'm away at boarding school. But I will never comp Brig on tickets when I make it to the NHL.

I feel a lot better when I look around. Dad was right; elbow grease was what was needed. And Brig was right; the house does seem welcoming. We close the door behind us.

"Let's roll." Dad hurries us to the truck. "We have a

field trip to catch up to, and we got off schedule." Jacob, Charlotte, and I roll our eyes. Even Brig says under his breath, "Not. Gonna. Happen." I feel another sting of jealousy that he knows Dad that well.

As we walk to the van, I swear the house sighs. I glance back and tell the house, "You'll see; it'll all work out."

Then I cross my fingers that my plan will turn out as good as the house.

ATTICUS AND CONOR

Atticus: I'm not happy that the boss left me in the van with the puppy when they stopped to get something to eat after we left the dirty house.

I don't bark and scratch at the windows and look pathetic when I'm left behind, like some people I know. I lie down on the seat and pretend to sleep because I have to be alert. You never know what might happen; strangers might try to touch the boss's van, and that's not going to happen while I'm around.

I have to growl at the puppy, because he tried to head-butt the door open and follow the boss. And he chewed on one of the seats until the stuffing came out.

But then my boy and the boss brought food and shared with me and the puppy. So did the muffin girl and the muffin girl's boy. I never eat any food from the boy who works with the boss.

Conor: I CAN HIGH-FIVE NOW!!!!!! Atticus fell asleep and was embarrassed when he woke up, but I kept watch. That's why I acted like I was trying to get out of the van—so he could do a good job and growl at me.

7

The Major Motion Picture
and the
Second Distraction

After we finished with the house, we grabbed something to eat, and by the time we left the restaurant, it was starting to get dark. It's all I can do not to cheer—a whole day wasted. Yay, me! Bobby Orr would be proud to share the ice with me. Motel, here we come.

"I feel like driving all night," Dad announces.

Say what?

"There's something magical about journeying on the open road under a starry sky." Dad looks around. "Heck, I might even write a country song while I drive! House flipper, songwriter—I like it."

No.

Nooooooo.

Nonononononono.

We have to spend the night nearby or we'll over-shoot the rink and tryouts.

I look out the window for a flea market or salvage yard. I've also got to figure out a way to get Dad out of the driver's seat. He can't notice the detour we need to take to get to the ice that holds my future.

I look at Dad singing and pounding on the steering wheel to the beat of the song blasting out of the radio. He's already made three or four course corrections since we got on the road this morning because he forgets about things like watching for his exit and highway numbers. He thinks he's got a much better sense of direction than he really does.

If only I could seize control of the wheel. But I haven't even taken driver's ed yet.

"So, Brig, got your license?" I cross my fingers. Dad's singing so loud he can't hear me over himself and the radio. Jacob is fiddling with the soft-serve machine, and Charlotte's reading and petting the border collies. I drag my eyes away from her. Focus, Ben.

"Sure." I gag as Brig mixes packets of honey and ketchup in a cup and then dunks pretzel rods.

"Does Dad let you drive the van?"

"Sure. Especially on garbage days, when I drive and he looks for stuff to rescue."

"Good times, I bet. Hey, don't you think it would be

a great idea to alternate driving with Dad? Give him a break?"

"Sure. I'll ask to switch now."

"Wait!" I grab his arm. This has to be a spontaneous event, a stealth attack.

Luckily, in addition to the aimlessness of Dad's driving, Conor needs a lot of pee breaks. That will be the perfect opportunity to switch drivers.

"Dad!" I holler over the music. "Conor has to pee. Keep an eye out for the next rest area."

Conor raises his head from his nap and looks at me, surprised. I can see the thought run through his mind: I have to pee? I feel bad lying to a puppy, so I rummage through my pockets, hoping there's a spare dog cookie to use as a bribe and an apology for using his weak bladder this way. He crunches happily. I love that border collies don't hold a grudge. Or tell on you.

A few minutes pass before Dad finds a gas station and Conor dutifully pees on the side of the road. I slip him another cookie. Atticus stares at me in disapproval because he can read my mind sometimes. "I don't care what you think. I'm doing it anyway." Atticus makes a noise that sounds like "hmh." Even though he doesn't speak, Atticus usually gets the last word. I try to give him a cookie, but he turns up his nose; Atticus cannot be bribed.

"Hey, Dad," I say oh-so-casually as we happen to be standing near the driver's door. "I could hear your phone buzzing with messages and emails all day. I know you're too conscientious a driver to check your phone when your eyes should be on the road, but it must be killing you to miss all that business." I pause to let that sink in. "How about Brig drives the next shift and you can sit in the back and answer some of those calls and messages? Maybe get some shut-eye?"

Dad leaps at the suggestion and Brig climbs into the driver's seat. I sit next to him, map in hand.

No one notices that I direct him to get back on the freeway, headed in the same direction we came from.

I shake off the guilt; soon I'll be enrolled in hockey academy and Dad will be ashamed of himself for putting me in such an awkward position.

I just hope I can keep everyone in the dark and time the drive right. And score a walk-on tryout. And dazzle the recruiters before Dad can shove me back into the van.

First things first: I need a good, lengthy distraction. Another one.

"STOP. THIS. VAN!" Jacob bellows from the seat next to the order window. He's hanging out the window waving and hollering, and all I can see from the front seat are his legs kicking and feet flailing inside the van.

It's freaking me out, like maybe we've lost a tire or are about to drive straight into a fiery inferno.

Even Dad looks alarmed. "Brig! Pull over!"

"What is it? What happened? What's wrong? Are you okay?" We bombard Jacob, and Atticus and Conor bark their heads off.

"Look!" Jacob's hand is shaking as he points across the highway.

It's a bunch of semis and trailers and—what is that? Gigantic silver umbrellas and miles of black cable all over the ground. No blazing fire or space alien landings. What is he so upset about?

"It's a movie set. They're setting up for an overnight shoot," he whispers. "Look: lights and generators and camera track and the mike boom. All I want in my whole entire life is to be in a movie. I just know I was born for it and that everything in my life has been leading to this moment. We've got to go over. Movie sets always need extras. I don't care if we just stand around and watch. Good thing I always carry my headshots; maybe I'll run into someone from casting."

Brilliant.

Jacob digs in his backpack and, sure enough, comes up with a stack of eight-by-ten glossy photographs. He thrusts them into Charlotte's hands and kicks off his hiking boots. "Avert your gaze," he instructs us. No one does, of course, and we watch as he kicks out of his cargo pants and replaces them with black suit pants and dress shoes from his bag. He rips off his T-shirt and slides into a white button-down with a necktie already looped through the collar, and a jacket that matches the pants. He travels with business clothes? That don't have a wrinkle on them? Man, I'm lucky if I have the right number of clean boxers.

"Let's go make dreams come true." Dad opens the van door and we all pile out.

"It's an intergalactic, postapocalyptic, war-of-the-zombies movie," Charlotte briefs Jacob, looking up from her tablet. "Loosely based on a bestselling graphic novel originally published in Japan and adapted by the guy who also wrote the screenplay for the totalitarian regime werewolf love story."

We all nod. Good stuff.

"They will totally want us to be extras," Jacob says, studying the set. "They don't have nearly enough dead bodies for an endgame scenario. And we already look horrible from cleaning the house!"

Dad lets the border collies out of the van as we head over to join a line forming near the set.

"Uh, Dad? Don't you think we should leave them here? We're gate-crashing a movie set, which is probably not proper etiquette. The guys will just call attention to us."

"No one will even notice them, Ben. Atticus and Conor are impeccably trained. It's like they're not even dogs. They won't bother anyone. Besides, every good movie needs man's best friend to really tug at the old heartstrings."

Atticus glares at me. I mouth, *I'm sorry,* and he tips his head in forgiveness. Then he glares at Dad for implying that he's a dog. But Dad doesn't notice.

Atticus is pretty stealthy and knows how to act cool, but Conor . . .

We take our places in the line of extras and slowly make our way to the front. Conor and Atticus stand next to Dad, holding their own leashes in their mouths. Dad thinks it's demeaning to them to be led around; he follows the law, more or less, by clipping leashes to their collars, but he refuses to hold the other end, so the border collies pick them up and carry them.

A woman with a clipboard, a headset, a walkie-talkie, and a ginormous cup of coffee hurries over.

"I'm the AD." She flips through papers on her clipboard.

"That's assistant director," Jacob whispers. "She's a goddess around here. All power flows through her. She's spotted my star potential."

I hope he's right. Plus, that would really help me out by killing some time.

"You can't have dogs on the set." The AD points to Conor and Atticus. "Allergies and biting are huge insurance liabilities."

"Atticus and Conor aren't allergic to anything," Dad tells her, "and I doubt the cast and crew of your movie struggle to control their impulse to bite." Dad cracks up. He thinks he's funnier than he really is and never got the memo that it's poor form to laugh at your own jokes.

I feel Jacob freeze next to me. I poke him so he'll hand the AD one of his headshots, but he can't move. He's got stage fright, or whatever fright it is when you need to make a good impression on the person who can get you in a movie and you can't do anything to prove your star quality.

The AD glares at Dad and stomps away in disgust. Jacob whimpers a little, the sound of a dream dying.

"Don't worry, Jacob. We'll think of something to get you noticed. Dad always says there's a solution to any problem. We just have to find it. He also says that two heads are better than one. And we've got five right here."

Before the five people can come up with any good ideas, one of the two border collies does. Conor hurls himself after the AD. I try to grab his leash, but he trots over to where she's standing in a huddle of people with clipboards and sits down at her feet.

I start to duck under the tape keeping us extras in a straight line to retrieve him before the AD notices him and has us thrown off the set, but I feel Atticus's teeth on my pants leg, holding me back. I trust him and stay put. Jacob, Dad, Brig, and Charlotte stand next to me, watching intently.

Conor starts leaning into the AD's leg, trying to get her to bend down and pet him. He's kind of spoiled that way—we've taught him that he's always going to be petted. The woman's ability to ignore affectionate puppies must really freak him out, because he pulls back and tips his head, studying her, wondering why she's not dropping to her knees, talking baby talk and kissing his nose, like some of us do, although I'll never admit to it publicly.

The great thing about border collies is that they are super determined to get their own way. Conor's ancestors moved huge herds of sheep across enormous fields and through numerous gates into specific pens with just a stern gaze and an obsession with pleasing their masters. One churlish movie person is no match for someone with his DNA. Conor stands up, puts his front paws on the side of her thigh, dips his head, and burrows his nose between her hand and her side, wiggling until she's passively petting him. He tosses his head, making her hand caress his ears.

I see her gently pat his head two or three times, tentatively.

She looks down at Conor and half smiles. He looks

intently into her eyes, then turns and stares at us and barks frantically. The AD glances at us and pauses, thinking, then points at Jacob. "Extra guy! The one in the suit, come over here. You can walk your dog through the shot as the zombies attack; it's not in the script, but it's a great image. I'm a brilliant filmmaker."

Jacob can only gape. Brig and I give him a mighty shove that propels him halfway to the AD. She grabs his arm and starts talking fast and pointing. She pulls a few pages from her clipboard and speaks into her walkie-talkie as she thrusts them into Jacob's hands.

Out of nowhere, another girl with a headset grabs Jacob's arm and hustles him and Conor into a semitruck marked MAKEUP.

"Hrf," I hear Atticus grunt, and I turn to look at him. For once, he seems to approve of Conor. He settles down to nap.

For the next hour, Dad, Brig, Charlotte, Atticus, and I are waiting for filming to start and watching the crew adjust the lighting as night falls. Charlotte reads us the cast and crew's credits, as well as reviews of the book the movie is based on. Brig eats a snack of fried pork rinds and black olives dipped in peanut butter; the rest of us edge away from him.

Jacob finally emerges from the makeup trailer, Conor trotting behind him. I only know it's Jacob by his suit;

his face is covered in zombie makeup. The makeup people worked on Conor, too; his fur is matted with mud. They run over to us.

"I only have a minute before we start shooting. I wanted to get some quick pictures with you while I'm in makeup."

We stagger to our feet, brush dust off our butts, and straighten our clothes.

Atticus always acts like he hates having his picture taken, but I notice that he's not pulling his face away when Jacob adjusts the angle of his nose and tells him, "That's it! That's your best side. Remember, now: always have them shoot you from the right."

Atticus snorts, but I make a mental note to take his picture later and see if he turns his right cheek to me, because I get the feeling Jacob has found Atticus's inner camera hog.

"Places, people. Scene twenty-six, invasion of the undead. Three-minute warning," booms over the sound system.

"I told you this was going to be the best day ever! But I didn't even tell you the best part!" Jacob is about to burst. "I have a speaking role: 'Oh my gosh, he ate her face!' I'll be in the credits! Screaming Zombie Number Eight."

We all cheer and follow Jacob and Conor on to the

set. Atticus cuts away, trots over to the AD, and sits next to her. "He's more of a behind-the-scenes guy," I tell Charlotte.

"Of course; Atticus's personality is better suited to production rather than talent." She watches Atticus study the activity around him and beams. "Like me. Jacob and Conor are the hams; we're the brains."

As Dad, Brig, Charlotte, and I are being directed to lie on the ground in various postures indicating a violent end, I try not to grin. A night of filming will put me on track to the tryouts. I know, I know—I'm acting shady. But then they have Charlotte lie so her head is resting on my chest. Her cheek rests on my sternum, and her hair smells amazing. I hope this shoot lasts all night long.

It's like Dad always says: sometimes the best way to solve a problem is to hand over a good idea to the universe and see what happens.

So far, so good.

ATTICUS AND CONOR

Atticus: Well, it's about time.

Just when I was trying to figure out how to leave him at the next rest stop, that puppy shows what he's made of.

I'm not convinced he knew what he was doing, but sometimes I wonder if there's more to him than he lets on. I hope so, because I'm going to need some help with my boy and the boss.

My boy has something on his mind. His eyes get dark and his mouth gets tight. And I don't like the way he glances at the boss and then the map or his phone real quick. I can't tell what he's thinking, but it's not good. My boy will need my help.

The boss notices my boy's face get dark; then he gets extra cheerful and fiddles with his phone. The boy didn't see the boss on the phone when everyone else was lying on the ground, pretending to be dead. But I see everything. I can tell the boss will need my help, too.

They'd be lost without me.

Conor: I DID GOOD TODAY!!!!!!

The Moment of Truth . . . and Consequences

One of the great things about hockey is that rinks usually open at five or five-thirty in the morning. Figure skaters and hockey players grow accustomed to being up and ready to function at what normal people call an ungodly hour, but normies have a hard time focusing at that time of the day.

Which is exactly what I'm counting on.

I turn in my seat and look at everyone.

After the shoot ended, Brig got his hands on a king-size cup of coffee at a gas station and dropped a glob of that chocolate-hazelnut spread in it to melt. He's over-caffeinating and oversugaring himself to stay alert as he drives. I'm getting used to Brig, if not his food, and I'm not going to freak out about him taking my place in the family until I get off the ice.

Charlotte's asleep on the floor between two benches, so I can't see her, but I can hear her breathe and I even think that's adorable. I might be falling for her, but I can't think about how to handle that until after tryouts.

Jacob is still sleeping on the far back bench. I get the feeling we could be buddies, unless he's the kind of guy who holds a grudge about being tricked into a secret plan. Still, I can't let this opportunity slip through my fingers because I might want to be friends with some guy.

Dad and Conor are fast asleep on one of the benches. Dad's going to be disappointed in me for scheming to take us off course and manipulating the situation for my own benefit. But I am destined to go to this hockey academy.

Atticus is staring at me from his seat near the order window. We nod at each other even though I'm pretty sure he knows I'm up to no good. I wonder if I should jettison the sneaky plan so no one ever realizes how calculating and self-involved I am.

I slap both of my cheeks briskly. Snap out of it. Pull it together. Take action. I have a plan; it'll all work out.

We're about thirty or forty minutes from the rink and I need to start getting dressed. Luckily, I have a lot of experience pulling on hockey gear in moving vehicles. Most people couldn't do it.

I pull on one long-sleeved and one short-sleeved

shirt. Since I know I'll be super nervous, I skip the long underwear—don't want to sweat myself dehydrated during tryouts. I also put on a jock and a cup, which are never skip-worthy. Ever. Even though they're super tricky to put on in a moving vehicle four feet from a girl. I pull on lightweight track pants as fast as I can.

I'm the kind of skater who doesn't wear socks—I like the feel of my sweat softening the leather of my skates and molding to the soles of my feet. It's an acquired taste. And it's a smell like the depths of hell. Even I think hockey skates are about the worst smell ever. So I pull on my team socks, which are really striped, footless tubes, over my shin guards, which I've strapped to my lower legs, and secure them with hockey tape wrapped around my thighs. I wrap more tape under my knees to help keep the shin guards in place.

Then come the hockey pants and belt; I'm not a suspenders kind of guy, although some old-school players swear by them.

I'm sweating buckets already and cursing our abundance of gear. This is always the moment where I second-guess my love of hockey. For a fast sport that makes greased lightning look sluggish, dressing for it takes forever. I bet even Mark Messier had trouble gearing up from time to time.

I won't put on my skates, elbow and shoulder pads, jersey, helmet, or gloves until I'm inside the rink and ready to take the ice with my stick. I'm so edgy, though, that I pop my mouth guard in. I look goofy, but at least I won't crack a molar grinding my teeth from stress.

Just in time. I see the signs for the rink, and as casually as I can manage, I spit out the mouth guard so I can tell Brig, "Take the next exit."

He glances over, does a double take—somehow he didn't noticed me gearing up eighteen inches away—and sends the van into a sickening swerve.

"It's a surprise; I'll explain to you and everyone in the back in a few minutes." I try to grin, but my mouth is so dry my top lip sticks to my mouth guard and I give more of a sick grimace.

"Uh-huh." His voice is flat. He should be thrilled I'm clearing the way for him to take over my place in the company. And the family. I feel a stab of jealousy.

Focus. Rid the mind of distractions.

I direct Brig to the rink and ask him to slow way down as he nears the front door. "Don't stop; I'll jump out and use my duffel to break my fall while you keep driving. Just circle the lot so the sensation of the van stopping won't wake anyone. I'll let you know when to stop."

He just stares out the windshield. After I've taken care of the registration details and am ready to get my skate on, I'll come back out and wave at Brig to park the van. And that's when I'll wake them all up and break the news to Dad.

I'm getting good at planning. Now I'm picturing Dad leaping onto the ice and sweeping me up in a big bear hug after I've flipped a puck into the goal past two big defensemen bearing down on me. I imagine a parade with confetti, and T-shirts with my name on them, and endorsement deals, especially for those protein bars and electrolyte water drinks I like. But that all comes after Dad says I was right about hockey school and assures me he totally understands, appreciates, and forgives my underhanded way of getting here.

Brig slows the van to the correct speed as we pull up to the rink. I tumble out, precisely as planned, on my pads and duffel, and roll to my feet. Man, where are random passersby with video cameras when you need them?

I sail into the rink and spot the sign-up table. My name is on their master list of invitees. I'm given a numbered sticker to put on my jersey and assigned to a scrimmage group. My age takes the ice in twenty minutes, so I put on the rest of my gear, except for my skates, which I leave loosened and ready to slip into next to my stick by the door to the ice. If you can't tighten and tie your skates in under a minute, you've got no business calling yourself a hockey player.

I'm ready to head outside to flag down Brig.

He sees me waving at him and slams on the brakes. Well, no need to worry about waking everyone; the way they were hurtled through the air did that nicely. I count to ten and head to the back of the van.

Dad, the guys, Jacob, and Charlotte look groggy. And, when they see me in full hockey attire, surprised. Dad and Atticus look disappointed.

"So, um, great news!" I say, adopting Dad's technique of fake cheer. "You all get to watch me try out for the hockey academy!"

I had planned to say more, but Dad and Atticus look away from me, and my mind goes blank.

"So . . . anyway . . . I'm up in a few minutes. . . . Hope you'll come in and, uh, cheer me on."

Silence.

I turn and trudge back to the rink. This isn't how I pictured this moment, and I sure never imagined the sinking feeling of . . . shame.

Then I start to get mad. This is all I want, all I've ever wanted, and Dad's ruining it for me. Again. First he yanked me out of camp last year after promising I could go, and now . . . I start to stomp a little harder.

Dad quits jobs and sells houses and reneges on promises and never asks anyone ahead of time if they're on board with his plans, and *he's* making *me* feel like a louse for doing what I need to do to protect the only thing I've ever worked for?

I jam my feet into my skates and yank the laces so hard as I tie my boots that I practically stop the blood flow to my toes. I stamp my feet a few times and slip my gloves on before pounding each fist in the other palm over and over. I'm mad now, really mad, and that's good.

I hear the whistle and I skate to my position.

The puck drops and the twenty minutes of our scrimmage whiz by. I can feel my blades shredding the ice, hear the thwack of the puck as it connects with my stick, taste the icy air I drag into my lungs past my minty mouth guard, see the black-and-white shirts of the refs as they zoom next to me along the boards. I can smell the fear of teammates and opponents who try to get between me and the puck.

I'm not usually a puck hog, but this morning I am on fire. Every player who's ever gone past the peewee leagues knows what it looks like when a fellow player is in the zone. You know better than to mess with it or water it down with thoughts of teamwork and good sportsmanship; you just get out of his way and let the magic happen.

All too soon, the final whistle sounds and the scrimmage is over. I realize I'm standing at center ice, clutching my stick and panting like a wild animal. Alone.

Dad's not sliding across the rink to lift me off my feet in a bear hug. Charlotte's not cheering from the stands. Jacob and Brig aren't hollering for me. The quiet hurts my ears.

So . . . no celebration. No bonding. No victory lap. I called this wrong.

I stare at the puck between my skates. The cold of the ice zings through me from the bottom of my feet to the top of my sweat-soaked head and I start shaking. I've shivered from cold before, but this is different. I stagger off the ice and head to the locker room.

No one speaks to me and I don't speak to anyone as I shuck my gear and let the hot water of the shower rinse away all my sweat. Guilt and dread stick around.

I towel off, get dressed, and shove my gear into my hockey bag, heading to the lobby. I don't see anyone from the van.

An official from the academy hurries over to me and hands me a stack of papers: the judges' comments on my performance. The reason I snuck here in the first place. The key to my future. I thank her and hurry out of the rink without catching anyone's eye or glancing at the papers. I can't wait to get away.

I thought I just wanted to go to the academy; I didn't realize until now that I wanted Dad's approval and support, too.

I scour the parking lot.

No van.

I drop my bag and try to catch my breath. This feels exactly like getting the wind knocked out of you by a high-sticking wingman.

I can't make my brain work, can't even begin to figure out how I'll get home from here or make things right with Dad. My eyes burn.

As I stare vacantly at the parking lot, a team bus pulls away. Behind it is a ratty van with a gigantic ice cream cone on top.

Dad is still here, waiting for me. I swipe at my eyes, grab my bag, and trudge to the van.

ATTICUS AND CONOR

Atticus: When my boy rolled out of the van—which I didn't like at all—and then came back and spoke to the boss, it wasn't a good thing.

The boss didn't say anything after my boy walked away. Then he said "No!" when the muffin girl tried to get out and follow my boy. She looked scared, and that's bad— the boss never scares people. So I barked at him and he apologized. But he didn't move, just sat staring at his phone. So I barked again. And again. And again. Until he finally looked up and said, "Oh, all right!" and went after my boy. I followed him and made sure he went in the building. I barked at the muffin girl and her boy and the boy who works for the boss until they went inside, too. I stayed outside, but I watched through the glass doors.

They all came out and got in the van, but things still aren't right; the boss and my boy aren't talking, but at least they're together.

Conor: I bit the boss's elbow. There's a little spot on the back of the arm where, if you nip real fast and sharp, it's enough to make them move. My boy wanted the boss to follow him, and Atticus was barking and barking, but the boss still wasn't moving. I nipped him. He moved.

He can start talking to my boy any time now.

The Make-Up Field Trip

Dad hasn't said a word since we left the rink.

Which is A-OK with me because I'm not speaking to him, either.

He's sitting in the far backseat texting, so I can't see him, and I won't turn around to look. Conor crawled into the footwell of the front passenger seat next to Charlotte's feet, and Atticus is staring out the order window. Even the guys are too disappointed to look me in the eye.

I'm sure Dad's not going to get me a puppy now, if he was planning to. It's clear he and the guys don't think I'm worthy of a puppy after the stunt I pulled.

Charlotte gives Brig directions in a soft voice and pets Conor. She hasn't smiled at me, hasn't looked my way since I climbed aboard at the rink.

Jacob fixed, filled, and started the soft-serve machine and hands out cones to everyone. I can't taste mine, but the burning, twisting, stabbing pain in my gut settles down.

Brig passed on a cone and is slurping from a stinky thermos cup of haggis or kimchi or something made of pickled ears and stuffed hooves. I once saw a guy in the locker room eat a sandwich that had fallen out of his duffel and landed on the shower floor, and even that wasn't nearly as gross as what Brig is eating now.

I finally get up the nerve to text Mom what I did. But I don't have the guts to leave my phone on to see if she responds. I'm sure she's already heard Dad's version. She and I always used to shake our heads together at Dad's crazy ideas, but ever since she started doing the books for the business and digging the house remodeling, it's like I don't know her anymore.

I glance at the critique on my scrimmage—great comments about my skills and hustle from every judge. I'm a shoo-in. Just like I planned. But I'm not even relieved.

I pick at the small tear in the left knee of my jeans until it's a gaping hole.

In my worst dreams, I couldn't have imagined such a crappy field trip. Which, by the way, isn't even happening. I knew Dad would forget all about getting Charlotte, Jacob, and me to . . . what was it again? No one has said a word about it since yesterday. We're just driving aimlessly at this point. I'd like to catch up with the field trip or else hurl myself out the order window, land on the roof of a semi, hold on until the driver stops to get gas, and then hitch home. Anything is better than being stuck in the Ice Cream Truck of Doom under the Death Cone.

"So, uh, hey . . ." Everyone jumps like I set off firecrackers. Probably because the speaker on the dash that blasts the ice cream truck song has turned itself on and I'm sitting next to the mike. My voice is blaring through the truck and out onto the freeway. The truck driver in the next lane swerves and then regains control before flipping us the bird and roaring off. Brig pounds on the dash until the speaker shuts off with a squeak.

"I, um, kind of lost track of the whole field trip thing. . . ." The tension in the truck is thick as we all think about why that is. "But, uh, what's the deal?"

"I was starting to wonder if anyone would ever ask," Charlotte says, "or if Jacob and I were the only ones who remembered why we hit the road in the first place."

"What's the field trip for, anyway?" Brig asks. "I just drive where you tell me. No one ever told me details."

"The rest of our class is going to a bunch of museums and on a tour of the government center to observe democracy in action," Jacob explains. "I know, totally dweeby. But you try arranging details for that many kids and finding enough chaperones and keeping the cost down and making it a cross-curriculum focus. Definitely not the best time ever. But it looks amazing on my resume."

"Jacob and I figured out we were never going to catch up with the class once we started working on the house," Charlotte explains. "So while I was emailing the foundation and the bank and waiting for their answers, I started brainstorming the independent study field trip Jacob suggested."

"And how's that working out?" Dad asks.

"Well! The movie set was a way better example of ego-driven power-mongers than any visit to city hall. So Jacob wrote a one-act play starring the two of us about power structures and decision making on the set. Boom! We've captured the spirit of democracy better than the field trip ever could."

"What about Ben? What'll he do?" Brig asks.

"Lie on the floor to reenact the pile of dead bodies. Teachers love visual aids and kids love dead bodies," Jacob says. "I can even tell them about the gut-sucking tube I learned about at the funeral!"

"Good thinking." I wish more school activities involved playing dead. Mom and Dad would never have anything to complain about, grade-wise.

"But that's not the best part!" Jacob says. "Tonight we fight for survival in the wilderness."

"Oh, uh, wow, that's . . ." I wish I'd never said I thought the field trip sounded boring. I may be a brute on the ice, but I'm not what you'd call outdoorsy.

"It's a forest preserve. We're camping overnight." Charlotte shoots Jacob a look. "We'll be there in a few minutes."

"How's that like going to a museum?" I don't get it.

"Our experience will help us as the founding members of our school's Eco-Preservation Society," Charlotte tells me. "We'll actively promote educational programs that advance environmental consciousness and facilitate public awareness with a call to action." She smiles. At me. I can't look away. Or feel my legs.

"See? It's not just *going* to a museum, like any boring schlub." Jacob bounces. "We'll *embody the spirit* of a museum. And then bring our knowledge back to school and share it with everyone. We'll save the planet, one middle-school student at a time."

"Uh-huh."

"We start by collecting examples of leaves and native grasses and flowers, identifying rocks and trees. Once it gets dark, we'll camp out, live off the land. I read a book about surviving in the woods; how hard can it be?"

I glance over at Dad; he's grinning. I've always thought he was waiting for a chance to see if he has what it takes to be one of those daredevil adventure guys. I guess I should be glad Charlotte and Jacob didn't think rappelling down the side of a cliff or skydiving was the perfect replacement for our field trip.

"Awesome. I've never been on a family campout before," Brig says.

"Very ... twinventive," I say, trying to look and sound as jazzed, or gullible, as everyone else.

"Here we are! Just pull up to any open campsite, Brig." Charlotte points.

"I'll go check in at the office." Dad whistles to Conor and Atticus. "You get started on your foraging and whatnot."

"I'll keep Mr. Duffy company," Brig says. "See if we can figure out how to make a shelter from all the tarps in the back of the truck, maybe rustle up some grub."

"No!" we all shriek.

"I'll drive back to the grocery store down the road while Brig sets up a shelter." Dad winks at us. "Get some hot dogs and buns."

I'm not sure how this counts as a field trip, but I don't mind walking with Charlotte in the woods. We let Jacob get a few feet ahead of us on the path and we walk side by side. Our hands brush against each other, and it's almost as good as stealing the puck. How did I never notice this girl before? Maybe Dad was on to something when he said hockey school would limit my options.

Maybe having friends instead of just teammates could be fun.

Jacob picks up every leaf and pebble and stick he thinks is pretty and keeps dragging me next to him for pictures in front of bushes and trees and flowers. "I'll just Photoshop some more normal headshots of you when we get home," he decides after scrolling through some images on his phone. "Because you still look like the undead from yesterday's zombie movie. A little dazed and out of it."

"That's because we're lost, and I'm dehydrated and starving."

Charlotte and Jacob argue about which way to head. "That's where we came from, Jacob. You are so wrong." And "It's clearly west. We need to bear west to get back to the campsite."

I'm about to lie down on the ground and expire for real.

"Arf." One terse, ticked-off bark.

Atticus is standing right in front of me, having appeared out of thin air. He looks annoyed and makes sure I understand he's here to save me and I'm meant to follow him before he turns and heads back down the path that neither Charlotte nor Jacob thought we should take.

"Oh, good, someone who knows his directions," Charlotte says, and starts to follow Atticus.

Jacob shrugs. "I'll follow Atticus anywhere."

"Arfarfarfarfarf!!!!" Conor comes tumbling through the woods, his fur covered in burrs, a small branch stuck to his collar. He hurls himself at me and propels me flat on my back. I can't breathe because he's sitting on my chest, licking my face and rubbing his prickly head on my chin. He won't stop barking and, oh, no. He just peed a little.

"All right, all right. Good job, you saved me. Stop peeing on my chest and go find Atticus."

He leaps off me and heads up the path Jacob wanted to take. I wait for a couple seconds and sure enough, a black-and-white blur comes hurtling back and zooms after Atticus. I follow more slowly. And find that Charlotte is waiting to walk with me.

When we finally stagger back to the campsite and spot the van, there's a line trailing away from our vehicle parked at the edge of the lot. Dad and Brig are studying the crowd. Jacob, Charlotte, and I walk up.

"Dad—what's going on?"

Atticus starts barking at the truck; he's looking up, barking at the Death Cone on the roof.

I laugh for the first time all day. "They're waiting for the ice cream truck to open."

"Good thing I fixed the soft-serve machine," Jacob says. "If we give the cones away, we can also add data about philanthropic efforts on the trip. No one on the official field trip will have done anything as cool as this. We rule!"

I scramble to find cones in the mess of boxes in the back. Then we take turns running the soft-serve machine to see who makes the best curlicue on top.

Jacob plugs the freezer in and does some tweaking to the motor and pretty soon it's humming away. "We'll fill it with frozen novelties later," Dad says. "Obviously, we have an obligation to carry treats."

"Obviously." But I smile. It was just a matter of time before Dad started selling ice cream. Dad smiles back and the chill between us warms up a little.

After the campers have all gone back to their campsites, we make dinner. Then Brig hangs tarps and rope between a tree and the Death Cone, and we have a funky tent. He says it's big enough for the four of us and the guys, but Atticus snorts and jumps into the van, making a bed from himself on the front passenger seat. Conor follows him. I follow the guys because they have more sense than Dad, Brig, and Jacob, who throw themselves under the tarp. Charlotte climbs into the van behind me, but Conor is in the middle seat between us and we can't even see each other because of the tall backs. It's still awesome that I get to sleep a few feet away from her.

The ice cream, the forest air and exercise, and listening to Charlotte breathe help take away some of my confusion about tryouts and Dad.

I wonder what Jacob thinks about tomorrow being the best day ever, because I feel about due.

ATTICUS AND CONOR

Atticus: We didn't go for a hike with the boss. I knew we wouldn't. We found a hammock and he took a nap. The boss is old now, and he needs more rest than he used to.

I didn't mind, though; the puppy is at his best when he's asleep.

I didn't nap. I sat underneath the boss to protect them. I might have closed my eyes for a second or two. I'm not so young, either.

Still, I can find my boy when he gets lost.

We're going to keep the muffin girl and her boy and the boy who works for the boss. They'll come to the house a lot and we'll get in the truck and go see them. And my boy will tell me stories about them and try to make me talk to them on the phone.

I wish there were another way to make friends like this that didn't involve bouncing in the van.

At least we didn't get a new puppy this time. That's progress.

Conor: I SAVED MY BOY!!! I had to pretend to chase a squirrel so Atticus could get to him first. I hope the boss didn't forget he's going to get me a puppy.

10

The Rescue

After the world's longest night, it's finally morning. We survived the wilderness. Or, in my case, sleeping in the van with farting border collies. We now possess the woods version of street cred. We're stiff and achy and we all smell a little funky, especially Brig, who reeks of vinegar, sour cream and onion potato chips and, I think, dead skunk.

Jacob and Charlotte agree that we surpassed the official field trip in terms of practical learning experiences.

"We are going to make everyone at school crazy with envy." Charlotte nods.

"If we head back now, we'll have time to get our homework done tonight," Jacob says. As if that's something to look forward to.

Dad takes the wheel and I sit in the passenger seat. I

wonder if we can start feeling more normal, maybe even talk about what happened. What comes next. Although I'm not going to start.

We've been driving for an hour or two on a smaller road; Dad likes to take country roads and back ways when he can. Atticus starts barking, jumping up and down, pawing at the order window, frantic to get out. He's never, ever, not once in my whole life acted like this. I can't remember seeing him so out of control.

Dad laughs and turns to me. "Border collies never forget anything. Ever." He turns into what looks like a farm and stops.

We get out and hear the world's most wonderful sound: barking dogs. Atticus runs to the enormous fenced-in yard and puts his paws up on the top rung of the fence so he can see better.

I've never seen anything so beautiful. Waves of rolling hills and grass waving in the wind and more dogs than I can count. Black and chocolate and golden Labs, beagles, pugs, Jack Russell terriers, retrievers, spaniels, a majestic-looking Irish setter; old dogs and young dogs; dogs that stand on their back legs at the fence, howling for us to pet them; shy dogs that peek around tree stumps; dogs that bark and yip and bray and howl and sing, begging us to play. It's a dog rescue. It's paradise.

My heart starts to feel warm and light just looking. Jacob and Brig and Charlotte are swept inside the gate by a worker who gives them buckets of dog food and water and points at the food bins scattered around the field. It's breakfast time, and every hand is a helping hand.

"This is where you got Atticus, isn't it?" Dad and I watch Atticus study the dogs running where he used to play.

"Yup. Couldn't think of a better place to find a puppy. C'mon. Let's see who's ready to be rescued."

Besides me. I hope a puppy will thaw the freeze between me and Dad. I sure don't know how to do it.

Dad heads toward the building marked Office and I follow, Conor at my heels.

This is where the puppies are kept. Dad and I inhale the amazing scent of baby dog.

I look at the row of crates against the wall and about fall over. A miniature Atticus and Conor is staring straight at me. Our eyes lock. Atticus and Conor and I love each other, but I feel totally different than I ever have before when I look in this puppy's bright brown eyes. I can tell he feels the same way about me. What they say about true love is right: you just know.

The puppy starts to wiggle, trying to get to me. It's crazy, I know, but I wish I weren't wearing jeans with a hole in the knee so I could make a good impression on this little guy.

Even though I know better, I unlatch the dog crate

without asking. The puppy leaps in my arms. We fit together. I sit on the floor and lean against the wall, holding him on my chest, our cheeks pressed against each other.

A lady wearing a shirt that says BYE BYE, DEATH ROW—HELLO, LIFE smiles at me as she walks by with a pile of towels. "Seems like you two were made for each other."

Brig, Jacob, and Charlotte walk in and stand next to Dad and Conor, watching me meet my puppy.

"What's his name?" I finally ask the rescue lady.

"I call him Puck. His litter all got Shakespearean names."

"It's a sign," Jacob says. "You play hockey and his name is Puck."

The lady nods; then she laughs. Atticus is standing at the door, waiting to be let inside. She pushes open the door and Atticus walks in, leans against her leg, and sighs. She must have been good to him when he was a puppy: he's grateful. I blink away a tear.

"Hello, my friend." She gets down on her hands and knees to hold his face. "You look good for an old man. I told you he'd take good care of you. I get your Christmas cards every year, so I know you've been well."

Conor starts yipping, jumping up to try to make me set the smaller version of him down so they can play.

Puck barks sharply and Conor drops his butt to the ground.

Dad laughs. "You've got yourself an alpha dog, son. He just let Conor know who's in charge."

I set Puck down and he touches noses with Conor. Then they both sneeze and Conor tips over.

Atticus groans and turns his face toward the door, as if he can't bear to look.

Dad calls Atticus to his side and ruffles his ears. "You'll see, it'll all work out."

But Atticus starts bumping his head against Dad's leg, trying to herd him away.

Dad looks down. "I'm telling you—it's all right. I never lie to you—you know that."

Atticus sighs and slinks over to the two pups. Conor looks nervous. Puck does a double take when he sees Atticus and quivers. But then he fluffs up the fur on his neck, trying to look bigger, and attempts to bark like he did at Conor. It comes out a yip. He looks embarrassed, backs up, scratches the ground like bulls do in the ring, tries again. This bark is better.

Atticus stops dead, blinks, and—I swear—chuckles, heh heh heh. His tail slowly wags and his ears go back as he sniffs the puppy from head to tail. Once he's found Puck acceptable from a smell point of view, he puts his nose in the puppy's ear and snuffles. Atticus-speak for "You'll do."

Conor has been watching intently. Now he launches himself at Atticus and Puck. He trips, of course, and knocks Puck over. Atticus forgets his dignity, sticks his butt in the air, tail wagging crazily, and barks as the two pups roll around, whining and yipping.

"This really and truly is the best day ever," Jacob says. We all grin and nod; he's right.

Dad starts to fill out the adoption paperwork while Jacob picks out a red leash and the lady helps Brig make a name tag. Charlotte and I read the ingredients on bags of puppy food and Puck gives some chew toys a test run. Brig hands me an ID tag: BEN'S BORDER COLLIE.

The lady takes our picture for her Web page. I keep an eye on Atticus while we're posing. He remembers Jacob's advice about his good side and leans forward with his right cheek.

Puck follows Atticus with his eyes; he knows Atticus is top dog. He yips at Conor and snaps at his back legs to keep him in line. Conor doesn't trip as much.

Dad and I take Atticus and Conor and Puck to the field behind the rescue building to play Frisbee before heading home.

Brig and Jacob are in a pen, covered in puppies. Charlotte, of course, has her tablet out. "I'm pairing the rescue people with local schoolkids who need volunteer hours." She gets cuter every time she has another great idea.

● ● ●

All three guys run off, about twenty-five yards, then turn and face us, dropping their chests to the ground, butts in the air, waiting. Dad flicks the disk in the air; Conor springs up and runs in the wrong direction, happy to bound in circles, barking. Puck sticks close to Atticus, who never takes his eyes off the Frisbee, waiting until the last possible moment to spring into action. He hurtles skyward, snatches the disk out of the air with his teeth, and runs back toward us as soon as his paws hit the ground, the puppy in his wake.

Atticus has never once handed me a ball or a Frisbee. He drops it three or four feet in front of me and then turns and runs as fast as he can to his waiting spot before I can pick it up and throw. No matter how many times you tell him "Bring it here" and hold out your hand, he won't do it. Dad says that we don't make the rules. It's Atticus's world; we just live here.

But Puck barks at Atticus when he does this and Atticus slinks over, picks up the Frisbee, and, for the first time in my life, hands it to me. Then, sulking, he lies down and pretends to nap while Puck and Conor race each other for the Frisbee and keep bringing it back to us. Dad and I flop on either side of Atticus and wait for the puppies to retrieve the Frisbee.

"So," Dad finally says.

"So." Here we go. The Talk.

"Your mother found us a house."

"She did? That's great." We won't have to kick Brig out of the van so we can sleep there. Whew.

"From the pictures she sent, I can see that it needs to be completely gutted."

"A lot of work?"

"Yup, it'll be a horrible living situation for a while."

"Good thing we're already used to that."

"You know it." He smiles.

"Why'd she buy a house in that condition, though? We need a break."

"To show me what it's like when someone makes life-altering family decisions without consulting the family. Kind of like what you did trying out for the hockey academy."

"Oh." I glance at him, afraid he'll look mad, but he smiles again.

"I get it now. How the two of you must have felt every time I made another big decision without talking to you first."

"It's a crummy feeling. On both sides. I know that now." I'm not going to have any jeans left by the end of this trip if I don't stop picking holes in them when I'm uncomfortable.

"We probably need to instigate a family policy so that doesn't happen again." Dad pats my shoulder. "You know, let's talk things over. I hear that works for some people."

"That'd be good."

Dad looks off. "Ben, I was wrong to decide not to let you go to the hockey academy the way I did, but I still don't think the decision itself was wrong."

"So the academy is really off the table? There's nothing I can say to change your mind?"

"The thing is—you'll be leaving home in four years anyway. And the academy is just getting started. And I know that any start-up has a lot of bugs to work out. I don't want them working them out on you. Meanwhile, you'll still play hockey. And high school in town could be great." He nods toward Charlotte on her tablet.

I'm surprised I'm not more bummed. I didn't think anything could mean more to me than hockey. Turns out there's more to life than what happens on the rink.

"Hey, Ben?"

"Yeah, Dad?"

"The other reason Mom bought the house is that it's a block away from the rink."

"You're kidding."

"Nope. Mom says you can see the Zamboni snow pile from your bedroom window."

"That's epic." The worst hassle about two-a-day practices and all those games has been trying to get rides; this is going to make my life amazing. I'll be able to walk over whenever I want, put in as much extra practice time as the rink has to give me. I'm still on the best travel team. I can go to school with Charlotte and I don't have to leave Puck. Or Atticus and Conor. And Dad and I are talking again.

Dad's not done. ". . . and I can't say anything until Mom calls back, but trust me; she's working on another plan you're going to like, one we've been talking about for nearly a year now."

"Mom has a plan?"

"Yeah. How Duffy of her, right?"

"I hope she's better at executing plans than you and I are."

"So do I, Son; so do I."

ATTICUS AND CONOR,
AND PUCK, TOO

Atticus: Another . . . puppy.

Conor: I GOT A PUPPY!!!!!

Puck: I got my boy. And a pack.

11

The Other Rescue

Atticus and Conor are trying to nudge Puck away from me in the backseat as we head home, Brig at the wheel. They think he belongs to them. But he barks, they back off, and he settles on my lap. I'd expect him to fall asleep—that's what puppies usually do—but he's keeping an eye on everyone in the van. He. Is. Awesome.

I suddenly realize I'm not obsessing about hockey. I can't remember the last time I wasn't stressing about injuries or running plays in my head or hoping my stick holds together for another game or plotting my next career move. It's kind of . . . relaxing. I'm enjoying the peace of mind, and I'm kind of dizzy because the sun lights up the little baby hairs near Charlotte's temple. "Things don't get better than this." I didn't mean to say that out loud, but a warm puppy on your lap is like truth serum.

"Brace yourself, Ben." Dad looks up from his phone.

"Huh?"

"Things are about to get better. Way better."

Brig high-fives him in the passenger seat. Jacob and Charlotte look back and grin. Everyone's in on something. Of course, I've been zoning out with the puppy, lost in my new Zen state, so it's possible they've been talking since we got in the van and I didn't hear a word.

"Ever since last summer, when I had to let you down about going to hockey camp, Mom and I have been working with your coach to pull together a summer training camp at our rink. Here." He hands me his phone so I can read what's on his screen.

My head almost explodes as I take it in.

"Twelve weeks of intensive training." I look up. "Real live NHL training staff and even a few retired pros!"

"You sound happy." Dad smiles.

"It's only twenty times better than the hockey camp I missed."

"I told you I'd make it up to you. I just needed a little time."

"I didn't think you and Mom cared about hockey or realized how good I am."

"We always knew. And I could see that you were one of the standouts in the scrimmage yesterday."

"You saw? I thought you stayed in the van. Actually . . . I freaked out that you might have left me there because of what a creep I'd been."

"I saw every second. A blur most of the time, but I knew: you were the one with the puck."

"We were way up high in the bleachers," Charlotte says. Charlotte saw me on the ice, too. If she didn't know about hockey before, I'm sure she's studied up on it since then and gets how killer I am on the ice. I hope.

"Way up high where the heat vents are." Jacob shivers.

"We sent Mom a video, so she saw, too." Brig waves his phone at me.

Mom, he called her. I take a moment to think about that. I don't feel jealous, so I tell him, "When I turn pro, I'll make sure you can get house tickets to every game. At cost."

"Frozen butts forever!" Brig yells.

Conor has to pee, so we stop at a rest area. Charlotte, Jacob, and I buy bottles of water; Brig chooses flaming hot corn chips, sour gummies, and malted milk balls.

The three of us exchange a look. Charlotte speaks for us: "I haven't wanted to be rude, but I have to ask— how can you stomach that crap you eat?"

"'Cause I'd be hurling," Jacob tells him. "You've downed some pretty gross combos."

"I was always hungry growing up," Brig says. "Never

enough food. Soda crackers and oatmeal, mostly, maybe some stuff in dented cans, whatever Mom could afford, whatever my dad didn't eat first."

Wow. Charlotte, Jacob, and I look at each other sadly.

Brig's eyes go dark and I get why he's so nuts about Dad, why he's always munching.

"Well, our dad doesn't roll like that," I tell him. "He always has our best interests at heart." Was it just two days ago he told me that and I rolled my eyes?

"He got some bad news before we left," Brig says. "He has to have the Calhoun place drywalled by Tuesday or the electricians won't be available. He's been trying to scramble a crew the past two days, but no one's available on such short notice."

Dad taught me how to put up drywall last summer. It's not hard once you know what you're doing.

"Even if we had five guys, we might not make it in time," Brig says.

"How about if you had twenty guys?"

"We could knock up those walls in a day or two if they were hard workers."

"They are." I rub my hands together like a cartoon character hatching an evil plot. "I need you to drive us somewhere without telling Dad, okay?"

Brig looks startled, but when I give him the address, he smiles and relaxes. "I'm in."

I hold my phone out so Charlotte and Jacob can see the text I'm starting to write, and they grin. "We're in, too," Charlotte says.

We climb back into the van. Brig drives and eats, and Dad dozes off with the guys. Charlotte, Jacob, and I send texts all the way home.

Except we head for the Calhoun place.

My hockey team and Mom are standing on the sidewalk.

Dad looks up with a start. "What?"

"Let's get to work," I tell him. "The guys are here to get the drywalling done pronto."

"You can't be serious."

"It's the least we can do; you set up hockey camp."

"And student government volunteers will be here soon to help paint and haul trash," Charlotte says.

"And when you're ready, the drama club and my track team are going to help you pack and move from the old house to the new one." Jacob high-fives Mom.

"Even though we're done with the field trip, the field trip's not done with us," Charlotte says. "We are on fire!"

"It's like I wrote in my field trip proposal"—Jacob grins—"'Planning for appropriate follow-up activities is essential and will facilitate student learning and multiply the value of hands-on experiences outside the classroom.'"

"You nailed it," I tell him.

After Mom hugs us all and shows Dad and me pictures of the new place—and Dad groans at all the work—she straps on her safety goggles and heads to the basement to start pounding drywall into place next to us.

"This might be the best trip we've ever taken, Ben." Dad and I watch my defensive line turn bare studs into walls. They work so fast it feels like we're in the middle of a time-lapse video.

"Like you say, everything always works out in the end. You always forget to mention the messy middle part, though."

"I don't forget. I'm smart enough not to talk about it because I'm waiting for the good part."

He can stop waiting; it's here.

ATTICUS AND CONOR, AND PUCK, TOO

Atticus: No one but me knows. Perfect.

That was probably my last road trip.

It's getting hard to keep up with the puppy and the new guy. My people haven't noticed that I move slower and my eyes are cloudy and, even though I pretend I'm just not listening, I can't hear as well. Pretty soon they'll start to compare me to the puppy and the new guy and it'll be obvious.

Even so, I like the new guy. He's more my style.

He's doing a good job with the old puppy. I knew it was a two-man job to train that one, but now I have help and everything's going to be fine. My boy says everyone needs a little assist once in a while. Even me.

It'll all work out.

Conor: I'm glad no one but me knows. Perfect.

Atticus is getting old.

He thinks I don't know that or how to do my job. I act goofy and clueless so I won't hurt his feelings and make him feel useless. I pretended I didn't see how hard it was for Atticus to jump up and down out of the van and to keep up with us.

Atticus would hate it if he knew I noticed anything. I can play along. I don't mind if he thinks I'm a goof.

I love the new guy.

He'll be a big help. Atticus is a two-man job, and we need to make sure he always feels like he's in charge.

I know it'll all work out.

Puck: I'm glad they don't know I know.

The old guy needs to see that I've got things under control. The other guy needs to think he's running the show. I know where I fit in and what my job is.

And I know that it'll all work out.

The Time After

We're having a last-day-of-summer barbecue this after-noon. At the new house. Or the uninhabitable money-sucking drain, as Dad calls it.

Dad complains, but he's having a blast. With help from the hockey team, and Charlotte and Jacob's team-mates and drama buddies, we're making great progress on our house. And we brought the Calhoun place in ahead of schedule and under budget; now Dad can pay everyone to work for him. He says they're the best crew he's ever worked with and he'll be sad when school starts.

Mom quit her old job and works full time for Duffy and Family. We changed the name of the company, since Mom's better at negotiating contracts and managing the crew. She's also pretty good at swinging a hammer; she's pitched in a few times when she thought people were slacking off.

Brig's not living in the van under the Death Cone anymore. Dad's first priority when we moved into the new house was to fix up an apartment above our garage for him—we would have given him a room in the house, but no matter how much we love Brig, we're afraid of what he might eat. Better he has his own kitchen. I got him a slow cooker and shared some of my recipes with him. Fingers crossed he starts eating better.

I don't know why I was ever jealous of Brig; he wasn't trying to take my place, just to find one of his own. One thing I know about this family—we always make room for someone who needs a forever home. And it's kind of cool to have a two-legged brother for a change.

Charlotte and Jacob are coming to the party, of course. Charlotte's been over a lot since we got home from the field trip. Which is totally awesome for reasons a gentleman keeps to himself. She's amazing and beautiful and she likes me back, so you do the math.

Charlotte worked it out so that we're going to surprise Jacob today with a DVD of our scene in the zombie movie where we're all a pile of the undead and he says his big line.

Jacob tried to get me to try out for the fall musical. I went to auditions with him, but I choked. Worked out okay in the end; I'm on the backstage and set crew for *Bye Bye Birdie,* starring Jacob Norton as Conrad Birdie.

The hockey team will come to the barbecue, too, along with the rest of the guys I met at hockey camp. I'm going to take lots of pictures tonight so when we all make it to the pros, I can show that we've known each other since we were kids.

Dad was right, and I don't even hate to admit it: Playing on the best hockey team in town, being a part of the world's most awesome hockey camp, working for the coolest family business in history, and having the greatest girlfriend ever is way better than obsessing about hockey 24/7/365. My feet smell better, too.

I still worry about my future, but now that just means I already locked down a date to homecoming this fall. Charlotte's teaching me to slow dance. Win/win for Ben.

The guys are really happy in the new house, especially since they spend most of their time in Brig's apartment to avoid the construction.

Atticus has really mellowed in his old age; or maybe it's having Puck around so he doesn't have to manage Conor on his own. I don't say anything to Dad or Mom about Atticus getting older; it would just upset them. Conor and Puck know what to do without me telling them. When Atticus naps, which is a lot these days, they curl up next to him, but they don't sleep, they keep guard. And they slow their steps so he can keep up.

I use some of the money I make at Duffy and Family to buy filet mignon and chicken breasts and those huge knuckle bones Atticus likes to chew. I act like I only buy the treats for Atticus, but I slip Conor and Puck their portions when Atticus isn't looking, and they're cool enough to eat them out of sight so Atticus feels special.

When I see that Atticus is changing, I'm glad all over again that I didn't leave home for hockey school. I've got forever to play hockey, but Atticus needs me now.

Dad still believes that everything will always work out. I believe that nothing ever happens like you think it will. But both of us know that real life is always a million times better than anything you can imagine.

About the Authors

Gary Paulsen is the distinguished author of many critically acclaimed books for young people, including three Newbery Honor Books: *The Winter Room, Hatchet,* and *Dogsong.* He won the Margaret A. Edwards Award given by the ALA for his lifetime achievement in young adult literature. Among his Random House books are *Road Trip* (written with his son, Jim Paulsen); *Family Ties; Vote; Crush; Flat Broke; Liar, Liar; Paintings from the Cave; Woods Runner; Masters of Disaster; Lawn Boy; Lawn Boy Returns; Notes from the Dog; Mudshark; The Legend of Bass Reeves; The Amazing Life of Birds; Molly McGinty Has a Really Good Day; How Angel Peterson Got His Name; Guts: The True Stories Behind* Hatchet *and the Brian Books; The Beet Fields; Soldier's Heart; Brian's Return, Brian's Winter,* and *Brian's Hunt* (companions to *Hatchet*); *Father Water, Mother Woods;* and five books about Francis Tucket's adventures in the Old West. Gary Paulsen has also published fiction and nonfiction for adults. He divides his time between his home in Alaska, his ranch in New Mexico, and his sailboat on the Pacific Ocean. You can visit him on the Web at GaryPaulsen.com.

Gary Paulsen is available for select speaking engagements. To inquire about a possible appearance, please contact the Penguin Random House Speakers Bureau at speakers@ penguinrandomhouse.com.

Jim Paulsen is a sculptor and former elementary school teacher. He lives with his wife and two children in Minnesota.